ketchup CLOUDS

ketchup
CLOUDS

A NOVEL BY
ANNABEL PITCHER

LITTLE, BROWN AND COMPANY
New York   Boston

Copyright © 2012 by Annabel Pitcher

Little, Brown and Company

Hachette Book Group
237 Park Avenue, New York, NY 10017
Visit our website at www.lb-teens.com

Little, Brown and Company is a division of Hachette Book Group, Inc.
The Little, Brown name and logo are trademarks of Hachette Book Group, Inc.

The publisher is not responsible for websites (or their content)
that are not owned by the publisher.

First U.S. Edition: November 2013
Originally published in Great Britain in 2012 by Orion Publishing Group

Library of Congress Cataloging-in-Publication Data

Pitcher, Annabel.
    Ketchup clouds : a novel / by Annabel Pitcher.—1st U.S. ed.
      p. cm.
    Originally published: London : Indigo, 2012.
    Summary: Zoe, a teenager in Bath, England, writes letters to a death row inmate in Texas, hoping to find comfort in sharing her guilty secret over the death of a friend with someone who can never tell her family.
    ISBN 978-0-316-24676-7
    1. Guilt—Juvenile fiction.   2. Grief—Juvenile fiction.   3. Families—England—Juvenile fiction.   4. Children's secrets—Juvenile fiction.   5. Epistolary fiction.   6. Bath (England)—Juvenile fiction.   7. Epistolary fiction. [1. Guilt—Fiction.   2. Grief—Fiction.   3. Family life—England—Fiction.   4. Secrets—Fiction.   5. Letters—Fiction.   6. Bath (England)—Fiction.   7. England—Fiction.]   I. Title.
    PZ7.P64268Ket 2013
    823.92—dc23
                                                                    2012044116

10   9   8   7   6   5   4   3   2   1

RRD-C

Printed in the United States of America

For my husband and best friend, Steve,
with all my love and heartfelt thanks

"How sad and bad and mad it was—
but then, how it was sweet!"

—Robert Browning, *Confessions*

S. Harris #993765
Polunsky Unit (Death Row)
Livingston, Texas 77351
USA
August 1

Dear Mr. S. Harris,

Ignore the blob of red in the top left corner. It's jam, not blood, though I don't think I need to tell you the difference. It wasn't your wife's jam the police found on your shoe.

The jam in the corner's from my sandwich. Homemade raspberry. Gran made it. She's been dead seven years, and making that jam was the last thing she did. Sort of. If you ignore the weeks she spent in the hospital attached to one of those heart things that goes *beep beep* if you're lucky or *beeeeeeeeeeeeeeeeeeeeeeeeeep* if you're not. That was the sound echoing around the hospital room seven years ago. *Beeeeeeeeeeeeeeeeeeeeeeeeeep*. My little sister was born six months later, and Dad named her after Gran. Dorothy

Constance. When Dad stopped grieving, he decided to shorten it. My sister is small and round so we ended up calling her Dot.

My other sister, Soph, is ten. They've both got long blond hair and green eyes and pointy noses, but Soph is tall and thin and darker-skinned, like Dot's been rolled out and crisped in the oven for ten minutes. I'm different. Brown hair. Brown eyes. Medium height. Medium weight. Ordinary, I suppose. To look at me, you'd never guess my secret.

I struggled to eat the sandwich in the end. The jam wasn't rotten or anything, because it lasts for years in sterilized jars. At least that's what Dad says when Mum turns up her nose. It's pointy, too. Her hair's the same color as my sisters' but shorter and a bit wavy. Dad's is more like mine, except with gray bits above his ears, and he's got this thing called heterochromia, which means one eye's brown but the other's lighter. Blue if it's bright outside, gray if it's overcast. The sky in a socket, I once said, and Dad got these dimples right in the middle of his cheeks, and I don't know if any of this really matters, but I suppose it's good to give you a picture of my family before I tell you what I came in here to say.

Because I am going to say it. I'm not sitting in this shed for the fun of it. It's bloody freezing and Mum would kill me if she knew I was out of bed, but it's a good place to write this letter, hidden away behind some trees. Don't ask me what type, but they've got big leaves that are rustling in the breeze. *Shhhh-wiiishhh.* Actually, that sounds nothing like them.

There's jam on my fingers so the pen's sticky. I bet the cats' whiskers are, too. Lloyd and Webber meowed as if they couldn't quite believe their luck that the sky was raining sandwiches when I chucked it over the hedge. I wasn't hungry anymore. In actual fact I never was, and if I'm being honest, I only made the sandwich in the first place to put off starting this letter. No offense or anything Mr. Harris. It's just difficult. And I'm tired. I haven't really slept since May 1.

There's no danger of me dropping off in here. The box of tiles is digging into my thighs, and a draft is blowing through a gap underneath the shed door. I need to get a move on because, just my luck, the flashlight is running out of battery. I tried holding it between my teeth, but my jaw started to ache so now it's balancing near a spiderweb on the windowsill. I don't normally sit in the shed, especially not at 2 AM, but tonight the voice in my head is louder than ever before. The images are more real, and my pulse is racing racing racing, and I bet if my heart was attached to one of those hospital things, all the fast thumping would break it.

When I got out of bed, my pajama top was sticking to my back, and my mouth was drier than probably a desert. That's when I put on my bathrobe and tiptoed outside because I knew it was time to write this letter. I can't keep it in anymore. I have to tell someone, and you're the person I chose.

I got your contact details off a Death Row website, and I found the website because of a nun, and that's not a sentence I ever thought I'd write, but then my life isn't exactly turning out the way I'd imagined. There was a picture of you looking friendly for someone in an orange jumpsuit with a shaved head, thick glasses, and a scar down one cheek. Yours wasn't the only

3

profile I clicked on. There are hundreds of criminals who want pen pals. Hundreds. But you stood out. All that stuff about your family disowning you so you haven't had any letters for eleven entire years. All that stuff about your guilt.

Not that I believe in God, but I went to confession to get rid of my guilt after triple-checking on Wikipedia that the priest wouldn't be able to say anything to the police. But when I sat down in the booth and saw his silhouette through the grille, I couldn't speak. There I was, about to confess to a man who'd never done anything wrong in his life, except for maybe having an extra sip of Communion wine on a bad day. Unless he was one of those priests who abuse children, in which case he would have known all about sin, but I couldn't be sure so I didn't risk it.

You're much safer. And you sort of remind me of Harry Potter to be honest. I loved those books when I was little. I can't remember when the first one came out, if it was before or after your murder trial, but anyway in case you're confused Harry Potter has a scar and glasses and you have a scar and glasses, and he never got any mail, either. But then all of a sudden he received a mysterious letter saying he was a wizard and his life was miraculously transformed.

Now, you're probably reading this in your cell thinking, *I wish this letter was about to tell* me *I had magical powers*, and if the website is anything to go by, I bet you're imagining healing every single one of those stab wounds in your wife. Well, sorry to disappoint you and all that, but I'm just an ordinary teenage girl, not the headmaster of a School of Witchcraft and Wizardry. Trust me, though, if this pen was a wand, then I'd give you the magic to bring your wife right back to life, because that is the thing we have in common.

I know what it's like.

Mine wasn't a woman. Mine was a boy. And I killed him three months ago exactly.

Do you want to know the worst thing? I got away with it. No one's found out that I'm responsible. No one has a clue and I'm walking around saying all the right things and doing all the right stuff, but inside I'm sort of screaming. I daren't tell Mum or Dad or my sisters, because I don't want to be disowned and I don't want to go to prison, even though I deserve it. So you see Mr. Harris I'm less brave than you, so don't feel too bad when you go for the lethal injection, which I wouldn't worry about, because when my dog was put to sleep, it really did look peaceful. The website says you'll never forgive yourself, but at least now you know there are people in the world far worse than you. You had the guts to own up to your mistake, but I'm too much of a coward even to reveal my real identity in a letter.

So yeah, you can call me Zoe. And let's pretend I live on Fiction Road, I don't know, somewhere near Bath, which is an old city with ancient buildings and lots of weekend tourists taking pictures of the bridge. Everything else I'll write will be the truth.

From, Zoe
1 Fiction Road
Bath, UK

S. Harris #993765

Polunsky Unit (Death Row)

Livingston, Texas 77351

USA

August 12

Dear Mr. Harris,

If you've opened this letter, I guess it means you're interested in what I have to say. That's nice but I'm not taking it as too much of a compliment, because let's be honest, you must be bored in that cell with nothing to do except write your poems, which by the way are really good, especially the sonnet about lethal injections. I read them on your profile and the one about the theater made me sad. I bet you had no idea when Dorothy followed the yellow-brick road that in forty-eight hours you were going to commit murder.

Funny I can write that almost without blinking. It would be different if I hadn't done it, too. Before, I might not have touched you with a barge pole, but now we're in the same boat. Exactly the same boat. You killed someone you were supposed to love and I killed someone I was supposed to love, and we both understand the pain and the fear and the sadness and the guilt and the hundred other feelings that don't even have a name in all of the English language.

Everyone thinks I'm grieving so they don't ask too many questions when I turn up looking pale and thin, with bags under my eyes, my hair hanging in greasy clumps. The other day, Mum forced me to get it cut. In the salon I stared at the customers, wondering how many of them had skeletons in the closet, because the nun said no one's perfect and everyone's got good and bad inside them. Everyone. Even people you don't expect to have a dark side, e.g., Barack Obama or Lisa from *The Simpsons*. I try to remember that when the guilt gets bad enough to stop me from sleeping. It didn't work tonight so here I am again, and it's just as cold but this time I've used Dad's old jacket to cover the gap underneath the shed door.

I can't remember the nun's name, but she had one of those raisin faces you could still imagine as a grape because somewhere underneath the wrinkles there was something beautiful. She came into my school a week before the summer holiday to tell us about capital punishment. When she spoke, it was in this quiet voice that wobbled around the edges, but everyone paid absolute attention. Even Adam. Normally he pushes back his chair and throws pen lids at girls' heads, but on that day we could take down our hoods because no one was doing anything they shouldn't, and we all gawped at this old lady as she told us about her work to abolish the death penalty.

7

She'd done a lot. Petitions and protests and articles in newspapers and letters to criminals, who'd written back and confided all sorts. "Like their crimes and stuff?" someone asked. The nun nodded. "Sometimes. Everyone needs to be heard."

That's when I had the idea, right there in the middle of the Religious Education classroom as the nun said a load more things I can't even remember. When I got home, I ran upstairs to the study without taking off my shoes even though Mum had just bought beige carpets. I turned on the computer and found a Death Row website, ticking the box that said *Yes, I am eighteen*. My lie didn't shut down the computer or set off an alarm. It took me straight to the database of criminals who want pen pals and there you were Mr. Harris, second man from the left on the third row of the fourth page, as if you were waiting to hear my story.

It all started a year ago with an unexpected phone call. For a whole week last August, I'd been plucking up the courage to ask Mum if I could go to a house party on a Saturday night. This house party wasn't just any house party, but Max Morgan's house party, and everyone was invited to mark the end of the summer because we were due back in school a couple of days later. Unfortunately the chances of Mum agreeing to let me go were less than 1 percent because back then she never let me do anything, not even shopping in town with Lauren, because she was worried about me being abducted and also about my homework.

There was no slacking off in our house because Mum quit

her job as a lawyer when Dot was little. She was a sickly baby, always in and out of the hospital, so I guess it was a full-time job to look after her. Mum was there when I woke up to ask what lessons I had that day, and she was there when I got home to supervise the work I had to do that night. The rest of the time she did chores. Because of the house's size, it was hard to keep it spick, never mind span, but Mum managed by sticking to a strict timetable. Even when she watched the news, she folded the laundry and paired the socks, and when she was supposed to be relaxing in the bath, she wiped the taps with a flannel to make them shine. She cooked a lot as well, always with the best ingredients. The eggs had to be free-range and the vegetables had to be organic and the cow had to have lived in the Garden of Eden or somewhere with no pollution and no chemicals so the meat wasn't contaminated with anything that could make us ill.

Mr. Harris I tried to Google your mum to find out if she was strict, making you try hard at school and be polite to your elders and stay out of trouble and eat all your greens. I hope not. It would be a shame to think you spent your teenage years munching broccoli now that you're locked up in a cell with no freedom to speak of. I hope you had some crazy times like sprinting naked through a neighbor's garden for a dare, which is what happened last year at Lauren's party after I'd gone home early. When Lauren told me about it at school, as per usual I put on my unimpressed face to show I was too mature for such things. But when my History teacher asked us to stop whispering and look at the worksheet, I didn't see the Nazis, just all these boobs boinging in the moonlight.

I was sick of missing out. Sick of listening to Lauren's stories. And jealous, really jealous, that I didn't have a few of my own. So when I was invited to Max's party a couple of months later, I made up my mind to ask Mum in a way that would make it impossible for her to refuse.

On Saturday morning I lay in bed trying to work out how to word the question before my shift at the library, where I stack shelves for three fifty an hour. That's when the phone started ringing. I could tell from Dad's voice it was serious so I climbed out of bed and went downstairs in my bathrobe, the exact same one I'm wearing right now, which FYI has red and black flowers and lace around the cuffs. A moment later, Dad was jumping into the BMW without even having breakfast and Mum was chasing after him onto the drive in an apron and yellow washing-up gloves.

"There's no need to rush off," she said, and Mr. Harris now we're getting into the proper conversations, I think I'll set them out properly to make them easier for you to read. Of course, I don't remember every single thing that everyone said so I'll paraphrase a bit and also miss out any of the boring stuff, i.e. anything at all about the weather.

"What's going on?" I asked, standing on the porch, probably with my face looking worried.

"At least have a slice of toast, Simon."

Dad shook his head. "We've got to go now. We don't know how long he's got."

"We?" Mum asked.

"You're coming, too, aren't you?"

"Let's think about this a minute."

"He might not have a minute! We need to get going."

"If you feel you have to go, I'm not going to stop you, but I'm staying here. You know how I feel about—"

"What's going on?" I said again. Louder this time. My face probably more worried. Not that my parents noticed.

Dad rubbed his temples, his fingers making circles in the patches of gray hair. "What do I say to him after all this time?"

Mum grimaced. "I've no idea."

"Who're you talking about?" I asked.

"Do you think he'll even let me in his room?" Dad went on.

"By the sound of it, he'll be in no fit state to know if you're there or not," Mum said.

"Who won't?" I asked, stepping onto the drive.

"Slippers!" Mum called.

I stepped back onto the porch and wiped my feet on the mat. "Will someone tell me what's going on?"

There was a pause. A long one.

"It's Grandpa," Dad said.

"He's had a stroke," Mum said.

"Oh," I said.

It wasn't the most sympathetic reaction, but in my defense I hadn't seen Grandpa for years. I remember being jealous of the wafer Dad received during Communion when Mum stopped us going up to the altar at Grandpa's church. And I remember playing with the hymn book, trying to snap it shut on Soph's fingers, humming the *Jaws* theme tune as Grandpa frowned. He had this big garden with huge sunflowers, and once I built a den in his garage and he gave me a bottle of flat lemonade to serve to my dolls. But then one day there was an argument and we never visited him again. I'm not sure what happened, but I do know we left Grandpa's without even having lunch. My stomach was rumbling, so for once we were allowed to eat at McDonald's and Mum was too distracted to stop me from ordering a Big Mac and extra-large fries.

"You're really going to stay here?" Dad said.

Mum adjusted the washing-up gloves on her hands. "Who else is going to look after the girls?"

"Me!" I said suddenly, because a plan had popped into my mind. "I can do it."

Mum frowned. "I don't think so."

"She's old enough," Dad said.

"But what if something goes wrong?"

Dad held up his phone. "I've got this."

"I don't know." Mum bit the inside of her cheek and stared at me. "What about your shift at the library?"

I shrugged. "I'll just ring and explain there's a family emergency."

"There you go," Dad said. "Sorted."

A bird flew onto the car hood. A song thrush. We watched it for a moment because it had a worm dangling from its beak, and then Dad looked at Mum and Mum looked at Dad and the bird fluttered off as I crossed my fingers behind my back.

"Listen, I really think I'm better off staying with the girls," Mum muttered without much conviction. "Soph's got to practice her piano scales and I wouldn't mind helping Dot with her—"

"Don't use them as an excuse, Jane!" Dad said. "It's obvious you don't want to come. At least have the guts to admit it."

"Fine! But it goes both ways, Simon. We both know your dad won't want me there."

"He'll be in no fit state to know if you're there or not," Dad replied, looking Mum straight in the eye. It was a clever tactic to repeat her words, and she knew it. With a defeated sigh, she turned toward the house, taking off the gloves.

"Have it your way, but I tell you now, I'm not going anywhere near his room," she said before disappearing through the front door.

Dad gritted his teeth, checking his watch. I walked over to the car, my fingers still crossed behind my back.

"So, do you think you'll be at the hospital for a while, then?"

Dad scratched the back of his neck and sighed. "Probably."

I smiled my most helpful smile. "Well, don't worry about us. We'll be fine."

"Thanks, pet."

"And I just won't go to the party if you're not back in time. It doesn't matter. I mean, Lauren will be disappointed, but she'll get over it."

I said it just like that—so off-the-cuff, Dad might think Mum had already agreed. He beeped the horn to tell her to hurry up.

"When does this party start?"

"Eight," I replied, my voice a little higher than normal.

"We should be home by then. . . . Hope so, anyway. I'll give you a lift if you want."

"Brilliant," I said, trying not to grin as I ran back inside the house.

In the afternoon Mum rang to let us know that Grandpa was stable and Dad was coping and they'd be back in time for dinner. Everything was turning out perfectly so I made myself an orange and lemonade with ice cubes that clinked against the glass. I spent the rest of the day in the garden, writing this kids' story called *Bizzle the Bazzlebog* because it's my ambition to be a children's author. In case you're wondering, Bizzle is a blue furry creature who lives in a tin of baked beans at the back of a family's food cupboard.

The story's supposed to be a fantasy for ten-year-olds and it probably sounds lame, but I enjoy doing it, pretending I'm still small and believe in magic or whatever. Anyway, I wrote for ages, then filled up the bird feeder that hung from the branch of a tree near the back door. Birds zoomed toward it—a magpie

that I saluted, a chaffinch landing on the ground, and a swallow swooping over the flower bed—and I watched them for ages, ridiculously happy, because birds are my thing and not to boast but I know pretty much every type in England.

I plucked a fat dandelion and twirled it between my fingers as I flopped onto the grass and put my feet on a plant pot. The sun in the sky was the exact same color as the flower in my hand and the two were linked by a hot beam of yellow. A bond blazed between them, and so yeah, it was probably just the start of sunburn on my knuckles, but for a moment it felt like me and the universe were connected in a giant join-the-dots puzzle. Everything had meaning and everything made sense, as if someone really was drawing my life by numbers.

Someone other than my little sister.

"Do you like it?"

Dot was standing over me in a pink dress, with a puzzle book tucked underneath her elbow, signing because she's deaf. I squinted at the picture. She'd joined the dots in the wrong order so the butterfly that was supposed to be soaring into the sky looked more like it was about to crash-land in the trees. I put the dandelion behind my ear.

"I love it."

"More than you love chocolate?"

"More than that," I signed.

"More than you love . . . ice cream?"

I pretended to think. "Well, it depends what flavor."

Dot dropped to her chubby knees. "Strawberry?"

"Definitely more than that."

15

"Banana?"

I shook my head. "Definitely not."

Dot started to giggle and leaned in close. "But really more than banana?"

I kissed her nose. "More than any flavor in the whole world."

Dot threw the puzzle book onto the grass and sprawled next to me, her long hair blowing in the breeze.

"You've got a dandelion behind your ear."

"I know."

"Why?"

"They're my favorite flowers," I lied.

"More than daffodils?"

"More than any flower in the entire universe," I signed, shortcutting the questions as the front door opened and footsteps sounded in the hall. I sat up, listening. Dot looked confused. "Mum and Dad," I explained.

Dot jumped to her feet, but something about my parents' voices made me grab her hand to stop her from running into the kitchen. They were arguing, the sound drifting through the open window. Before they had the chance to realize I was there, I ducked behind a bush, pulling Dot after me. She laughed, thinking it was some sort of game, as I parted the leaves.

Mum banged a cup on the kitchen counter. "I can't believe you agreed to it!"

"What was I supposed to do?"

She jabbed the switch on the kettle. "Talk about it with me! Discuss it!"

"How could I when you weren't even in the room?"

"That's no excuse."

"He's their grandfather, Jane. He has a right to see them."

"Don't give me that! They've had nothing to do with him for years."

"All the more reason for them to spend time with him now, before it's too late."

I watched Mum roll her eyes as I tried to keep hold of Dot, who was twisting and turning, trying to get free. Putting my hand over her mouth, I did a *shush* face with very stern eyebrows. In the kitchen, Mum grabbed a teaspoon out of the drawer, banging it shut with her hip.

"We made a decision about this years ago. Years. I'm not going back on it now just because your father's a little bit—"

"He's had a stroke!"

Mum flung the teaspoon into the cup. "That doesn't change a thing! Not one thing! Whose side are you on?"

"I don't want there to be any sides, Jane. Not anymore. We're a family."

"Try telling that to your—" Mum started, but just at that moment, Dot bit my finger and broke free and there was absolutely nothing I could do about it. She ran off as fast as she could and did two cartwheels on the lawn. Her dress fell around her shoulders, showing off her knickers, and she ended up in a big heap on the grass. As Mum and Dad stared out the window, Dot picked a dandelion. Only this one was white. Fluffy. Full of those wispy things that look like dead fairies. The sun disappeared behind a cloud as Dot blew hard and the dandelion vanished, and Mr. Harris I'm going to stop writing

17

now because I'm tired, plus I've got pins and needles in my left leg.

From,
Zoe
1 Fiction Road
Bath, UK

S. Harris #993765

Polunsky Unit (Death Row)

Livingston, Texas 77351

USA

September 2

Dear Mr. Harris,

The best thing about this shed is definitely the lack of eyes. No eyes at all apart from eight on the spider, and they're not looking at me. The spider's in the web on the windowsill, staring through the glass at the silhouette of the tree and the cloud and the half-moon, silver reflected in her eyes as she thinks about flies or whatever.

It'll be different tomorrow. The eyes will be back. Sad ones and inquisitive ones and some that stare and others that try not to look but keep on glancing as I walk into school to start the new term. There'll be nowhere to hide, not even the toilets if that's what you're thinking, because last term some girls waited for me to come out of a stall then pounced on me, wanting to know everything—what and when and where and how but not who, because they'd all been to his funeral.

Questions questions questions questions getting louder and louder just like that and I didn't know what to say. My back started to sweat, a hot white bone burning from my bum to my brain. I turned on the tap as far as it would go. Water gushed over my hands trying to wash away the guilt. I started to scrub harder and harder as my breath came quicker and quicker and the girls moved closer and closer, and I couldn't stand it for a second longer so I ran for it. Barging through the door, I collided with my English teacher, who took one look at my face and ushered me into her office.

On the wall there was a picture of Lady Macbeth above the quote "Out, damned spot," and Mr. Harris I don't know if you're familiar with Shakespeare but in case you're wondering, Lady Macbeth wasn't banging on about a pimple on her chin. I stared at Lady Macbeth's bloody hands as my own shook violently. Mrs. Macklin cooed, "There there don't worry there's no rush take as long as you need," and I wondered if she actually meant it, if it would be okay for me to sit at her desk next to her pile of marking till the end of time. I couldn't stand her being nice, patting my arm and telling me to breathe, saying I was doing so well and I was so brave and that she was so sorry, for all the world as if it were her fault, not mine, that his body is in a coffin.

That's the hardest thing of all—the knowledge that he's under the ground. With his eyes wide open. Brown eyes that I know so well, staring up at the world they can no longer reach. His mouth's open, too, like he's screaming the truth but no one can hear. Sometimes I even see his fingernails, bleeding and torn because he's been scratching words into the coffin lid, this long explanation of what happened on May 1, buried six feet under so no one will ever read it.

But maybe these letters are helping Mr. Harris. Maybe as I get more and more of the story to you, more and more of the story will disappear from the coffin until it's all gone for good. His fingernails will heal and he'll cross his hands on his chest and close his eyes at long last, and then the maggots will come to eat his flesh but it will be a relief and his skeleton will smile.

That's a reassuring thought but I suppose I'd better get back to telling you what happened last year after Mum and Dad had the argument about Grandpa. From what I can remember, they were trying to act normal after their fight but there was tension I could have cut with my knife, which probably would have been easier than slicing through the steak on my plate. Mum never normally made a mess of the food but that night everything was overcooked. I hope I don't sound ungrateful Mr. Harris. I mean, you must be sick of prison meals, which I imagine to be some sort of gruel as seen in the musical *Oliver!* Maybe the guards eat pizza right in front of your cell, so close you can smell it, and it's all you can do not to start singing "Food, Glorious Food" in a cockney accent.

If it's any consolation, the food Mum cooked that night wasn't the slightest bit glorious and we gave up on the steak after five minutes.

"Why haven't I met Grandpa before?" Dot signed suddenly.

Dad picked up his wineglass but didn't take a sip.

"You have, my love," Mum signed. "You just don't remember."

"Did I like him?"

"You . . . well, you were too young to have an opinion," Mum replied.

"Is he going to be okay?"

"We hope so. He's very ill, though."

"Will he be okay tomorrow? Or the next day? Or the day after that?"

"Stop asking stupid questions," Soph muttered. Dot stared at her blankly because she struggles to lip-read. "Stop asking stupid questions," Soph said again, moving her lips even faster on purpose.

"*Sophie*," Mum warned.

"Grandpa's going to be fine, pet," Dad signed, his hands slow and clumsy. "He's in the hospital but he's stable."

Mum put her arm around Dot's shoulders and nuzzled the top of her head. "Don't worry."

"I'm worried, too," Soph announced suddenly. "Like what if he *dies* or something."

Dad sighed. "Don't be dramatic."

I glanced at the grandfather clock. Forty-five minutes until the party started. I started to whistle. I never normally whistled. Mum watched me suspiciously as I took my plates to the sink, my bare feet cold against the tiles.

"Where're you going?" she asked.

I didn't dare look at her. "To get ready."

"For what?"

Dropping my knife and fork into the water, I stared at the bubbles. "The party at Max's house."

"What party? What party, Zoe?"

I spun around. "Dad said I could go!"

Mum glared at Dad as he dipped his finger into some ketchup on his plate and licked it clean. "Well, she's been good all day." It was more than I could have hoped for. I had to fight the urge to run over and kiss him.

"Were you going to mention it to me, Simon?"

"I don't have to run every decision by you."

"Oh, so this is how it's going to be from now on, is it?" Mum flared up. "You making decisions—ridiculous decisions—that affect the whole family, without considering—"

Dad's cheeks flushed. "Don't start all that again, Jane. Not in front of the girls."

Mum exhaled noisily, but she dropped the subject. I moved to the kitchen door as Dot picked up a green bean and threw it back onto her plate in the manner of a javelin.

"Gold at the Olympics!" she signed. "And gold in the shot put!" She chucked a carrot. It bounced off Soph's elbow and landed next to the salt pot.

"Mum, will you tell her?" Soph moaned.

"Stop it, girls," Dad snapped.

"Why are you having a go at me?" she exploded.

"Leave it, Soph," Mum said.

"This is so unfair!" she cried, flinging a hand into the air and accidentally hitting a glass. It flew across the table, black currant juice spilling everywhere. Dad swore as Mum leaped up to grab a tea towel.

"So can I go, then?" I asked.

"No!" Mum said.

"Yes!" Dad said at the same time.

They glowered at each other as black currant dripped onto the floor.

"Fine!" Mum snapped. "But I'm picking you up at eleven."

Before Mum could change her mind, I charged out of the kitchen and raced up the stairs two at a time, bursting into my bedroom. It was tidy, of course, because Mum made me keep it that way, my clothes hanging neatly in my closet and my purple duvet completely straight. My lamp stood in the exact middle of my bedside table, and on the shelf above my headboard, my books were stacked so all the titles faced the same way. Only my desk was messy, pages of *Bizzle the Bazzlebog* spread all over it, Post-it notes stuck to my bulletin board with details of characters and plot twists scribbled in pen.

I got ready quicker than ever in my life, pulling on a pair of black jeans and a top. Really I should have washed my hair but Mr. Harris there wasn't time so I tied it back in a messy ponytail, then put on a pair of earrings, nothing fancy or girly, just plain silver hoops. Before I ran out of my bedroom, I slipped on a pair of flat shoes, then hopped into Dad's car.

We heard the house before we saw it, all this music, heavy beats throbbing in the air. Dad pulled up near a row of terraces.

They were small and simple, pretty much how Dot would draw a house if I gave her a crayon and a piece of paper. Two windows at the top. Two at the bottom. A front door in the middle and a long, thin garden with one tree next to a straight path half covered in grass.

Balloons in the shape of beer bottles bobbed about in the distance, silver strings tied to the gate at the very end of the row. I climbed out of the car, my face probably pink and my mouth definitely dry, because I remember struggling to swallow without any spit.

"Be good, eh?" Dad said, catching sight of the balloons. "I could do without any more drama today."

He sounded so fed up, I stuck my head back through the door. "You okay?"

A yawn. A flash of fillings. "I'll be fine."

"Grandpa's going to get better, you know."

Dad gazed out of the window without seeing the group of girls stumbling past in dresses and high heels. Four inches, they must have been, and I suddenly wondered if I looked ridiculous in my flat shoes and jeans.

"He just seemed so . . . oh, I don't know. Old, I suppose."

I stared down at my feet, trying to imagine them from someone else's perspective. "He *is* old, Dad."

"He used to run marathons."

I looked up, surprised. "Really?"

"Oh yeah. He was fit. He did it in just over three hours once."

"Is that good?"

Dad smiled, but it was sad. "It's more than good, pet. And he could dance. Gran, too. They were quite something."

The music in the house got louder. Dad was far away in his thoughts but the party was right there in front of me, and I didn't want to be rude but time was ticking ticking ticking. When enough seconds had passed, I leaned into the car and pecked him on the cheek before setting off, wondering what music Grandpa had liked and how he had looked, dancing with a body as young as mine.

Just because I could, just because I wasn't stiff or frail or stuck in the hospital after a stroke, I sped up, grateful for my working limbs and moving joints and the fact that I wasn't old. By the time I reached the end terrace, my pulse was racing. The front door was open, people making their way inside. I paused by the gate, batting the balloons to one side, taking it all in, and honest truth, it looked like a whole new world and not just a hall with an old blue carpet. My stomach fluttered and my adrenaline tingled and I felt young Mr. Harris, really young in this precious sort of way. I savored the moment, then hurried up the path, avoiding the cracks between the slabs.

"Stepping-stones over a fast river? Or hurdles in the Olympics?"

A boy I didn't recognize was sitting on a bench in the front garden. Brown eyes. Messy blond hair that looked as if it had never been brushed. Tall enough. Lean. "What were you imagining?" he called over the music, pointing at the cracks.

I shrugged. "Nothing. I'm superstitious, that's all. If you tread on the cracks it's bad luck, isn't it?"

The boy looked away. "Disappointing."

"Disappointing?"

"I thought you were playing a game."

"I can play a game if you want me to play a game," I replied. My voice surprised me. Confident. Flirtatious, even. A brand-new sound.

The boy looked back, interested now. "Okay. Here's a question. If the cracks were something dangerous, what would they be?"

I thought for a moment as three girls tottered into the party, smirking at my outfit. "Mousetraps," I replied, trying to ignore them.

"Mousetraps? You can have any fantasy in the whole world, and you choose *mousetraps*?"

"Yeah, well . . ."

"Not alligators or deep black holes with snakes at the bottom. Tiny little mousetraps with bits of cheddar stuck on the snappy thing."

I took a step closer, then another, enjoying myself immensely. "Who said they're *tiny* mousetraps?" I prodded the cracks with the end of my shoe. "Maybe they're huge ones with poisonous cheese and spikes that can rip my toes to shreds."

"Are they?"

I hesitated. Then smiled. "No. They're tiny little mouse-traps with bits of cheddar stuck on the snappy thing."

Above our heads, something flew into a tree and hooted.

"Owl!" I exclaimed.

The boy shook his head. "There you go again."

27

"There I go what?"

Sighing, he stood up. His shoulders were wide as if they could carry the weight of the whole world or at least give me a good piggyback. He was wearing faded blue jeans and a black T-shirt that bagged in all the wrong places. He'd made even less effort than me. All of a sudden my flat shoes seemed to float four inches off the ground.

"Can you see the bird?" he asked, putting his hand over his eyes and gazing into the leaves.

"Well, no, but—"

"So how do you know it's an owl? It could have been a ghost."

"It's not a ghost."

The boy walked toward me and my breath caught in my throat. "But how do you know? It could have been a spirit that—"

"I know it's an owl because of the hoot," I interrupted. The bird did it again, right on cue. I held up my finger. "Hear that? That's the cry of the little owl. The mating cry, actually."

The boy raised an eyebrow. I'd surprised him.

"The mating cry, huh?" His eyes twinkled and I felt triumphant. "Tell me more about this amorous little owl."

"Well, it's one of the most common species in Britain. And it has feathers. Obviously," I said, feeling self-conscious. "But they're beautiful, sort of speckled, brown and white. It's got a big head, long legs, yellowish eyes," I went on, warming to my theme, "and this bounding, undulating sort of fly, similar to a woodpecker, really, and . . ."

The boy started to laugh. Then I started to laugh. And then the owl hooted as if it was starting to laugh.

"What's your name?" he asked, and I was just about to reply when the gate creaked and heels tapped up the path.

"Bloody hell, you actually came!" Lauren shrieked. "Let's get a drink!" Before I could protest, she grabbed my hand and tugged me toward the house, stumbling on a crack.

"Mind the alligators," I said. Out of the corner of my eye, I saw the boy grin.

Lauren stopped, looking confused. "What?"

"Doesn't matter," I muttered, and then I grinned, too.

The living room was small with a faded red carpet and a beige sofa pushed to one side to make room for dancing. Lauren threw off her coat and joined in, all *Wooooo* and waving her arms in the air. She twirled in the middle of the room as I grabbed a glass off the drinks table and poured myself some lemonade. And then, after a pause, some vodka. I mixed it with my finger, music pounding in my ears and my blood and every single one of my organs. *La la la la la*, my heart sang, just like that. I downed my drink in one as people gyrated between the sofa and the mantelpiece as if they were in a nightclub rather than a living room, and honest truth they looked ridiculous, grinding against each other on the rug.

And then all of a sudden there he was, leaning against the door frame, amused by the scene. He caught my eye or maybe I caught his, or possibly they caught each other at the exact same moment. As everyone danced, he shook his head and I rolled my eyes, and we both knew exactly what the other was thinking, like imagine our heads connected by a telephone wire. The boy didn't move toward me and I didn't move toward him, but that cable between our brains buzzzzzzed.

Someone with ginger hair got in the way, but the boy kept glancing at me and glancing at me as if I was worth a second and a third and a one-hundredth look. My body felt different under his gaze. Not just arms and legs and bones. Skin and lips and curves. I poured myself another drink as the boy chatted to his friend. My hands were unsteady. Lots of vodka went in my glass but lots splashed on the table. Cursing, I grabbed a napkin, and by the time I'd cleaned it up, the boy had disappeared. Just like that. One second he was by the door, and the next he wasn't, and my heart stopped dead with a big fat *Oh*.

I told Lauren I was going to the bathroom and took off at once, squeezing past bodies and ducking under arms into the hall. He wasn't outside or in the kitchen or in the cupboard full of coats. Pushing past people on the narrow stairs, I swigged my drink, opening three doors to find nothing but empty rooms. I tried the upstairs bathroom. The downstairs, too, filling my glass on the way there, just neat vodka this time, and I swallowed it in one go as I tried the handle.

It turned easily to reveal a dripping tap and a toilet, and I gazed at my frowning face in the mirror, my reflection swimming in and out of my vision as I gripped the edges of the sink. I steadied myself, then stumbled into a tiny sunroom. It was big and cool and dark, just the moon shining through the glass ceiling. In the far corner was a comfy-looking chair and I fell into it as the room started to spin. As my bum touched the cushion, a voice said, "Hey."

My head jerked up, but it wasn't the boy, Mr. Harris. It was Max Morgan. *The* Max Morgan. And he was grinning at me, a bottle of whiskey in his hand. Drink was splashed down his smart shirt and his forehead was shiny with sweat, but his eyes were brown, really brown, and his short hair was dark and styled, and his grin was crooked in a way that sent me all off-kilter.

"Hey," Max said again. "Hannah?"

"Zoe," I replied. Except of course I didn't. I used my real name, the one I can't tell you.

"Zoe," Max repeated. "Zoe Zoe Zoe." He burped behind closed lips then let it out slowly. He pointed at my chest suddenly. "You're in my French class!"

"No."

Max held up his hands and almost fell over. "Sorry. Sorry sorry. You just look like someone I know."

"We've been at the same school for three years."

Max completely missed my tone. "Is it me or is it really hot in here?" He stumbled toward the sunroom door and tried to open it. "This is broken. Hannah, it's broken."

I climbed to my feet and turned the key. "It's Zoe, and it's fixed."

Max hiccupped. "My hero. Heroine. Like the drug." He pretended to put a syringe in his arm then laughed at his own joke, holding out the bottle. "Drink?" I made to grab it, but Max jerked the bottle out of my reach then stepped outside. "You coming?"

The night was warm, perfect for sitting in. A breeze lifted my hair as Max took my hand. My stomach flipped over as our fingers interlinked and I wondered what Lauren would say if she could see Max Morgan's thumb rubbing one of my knuckles. I thought about telling the story on Monday morning. *And then Max led me to a stone fountain at the bottom of the back garden. A moth was floating in the water. Max touched it gently with the very tip of his finger before lowering himself onto the grass. Swigging the whiskey, he looked up at me and I looked down at him, and we both knew that something incredible was about to—*

Max belched.

"You just going to stand there or what?"

I sat down as he handed me the bottle. One more sip couldn't hurt. That's what I told myself. That's what I told myself every single time Max held out the bottle, the rim shining in the moonlight, wet with spit. He put his hand on my leg, and I didn't stop it, not even when it crept up my thigh. At some point I started talking about Grandpa, and how he was ill, and how he'd been in shape when he was young.

"I'm in shape," Max said, and then he hiccupped.

"They were quite something, my grandparents," I added, and I remember having to work really hard to stop my words from slurring.

"My parents were, too. Before. Not now. They don't even speak anymore."

"They were also really good at dancing," I went on, weaving my hands together to show what I meant.

"I'm good at dancing," Max said, nodding too hard, his head going up and down in the darkness. "Really good."

"Yeah, you are," I replied solemnly, though I had absolutely no idea. "And my grandparents were young once. Young. Don't you think that's weird?"

Max hiccupped again and tried to focus on my face. "We're young. We're young right now."

"True," I said. "Very true." It was the wisest conversation anyone had ever had and I smiled wisely because of my great wisdom and also possibly because of the whiskey. Max leaned in close, his nose brushing against my cheek.

"You're nice, Zoe," he said, and because he got my name right, I kissed him on the lips.

Now, Mr. Harris, you're probably shifting about on your bed feeling awkward about what's going to happen next and I bet you anything your mattress squeaks because a criminal's comfort is not going to be high on the list of priorities for jail funding when there are inmates trying to escape. Not you, though. I reckon you're just sitting in your cell, accepting your fate, because you think you deserve to die. You sort of remind me of Jesus, to be honest. You have to bear sins and he had to bear sins, only his were heavier. I mean, imagine the weight of all the sins of the world.

If you could actually measure it, pouring out sins on the scales like self-rising flour, I have no idea what the heaviest crime would be, but I don't think it would be yours. I reckon a lot of men would have done the same after what your wife told you. Think about that when you feel guilty. A couple of months ago, I printed off this list of all the men responsible for genocide, and at night when I can't sleep, instead of counting sheep, I count dictators. I send them leaping over a wall, Hitler and Stalin and Saddam Hussein jumping through the air in their uniforms with their dark mustaches blowing in the breeze. Maybe you should try it.

I tell myself I couldn't have known what was going to happen a year ago when Max put his arm around me in the garden. I try to remember how I was swept along in the moment, barely able to walk straight as Max ushered me inside, through the house, and upstairs to his bedroom. It smelled of dust and feet and aftershave. Max flicked on the light and closed the door as I stepped over a pair of boxer shorts crumpled up on the carpet.

Hitler jumping over a wall

A hand on my back pushed me toward the wall. I glanced over my shoulder to see Max smile. He pushed harder. My hands touched the wall, then my body, then my head, all pressed up against a poster of a naked woman. The poster was cool so I rested my forehead against the model's belly as Max kissed my neck. It was tingly, like if electricity had a mouth, then that is exactly how it would have felt.

That was the spark and we exploded into action, hands grabbing and lips hungry and breath quick and fast in our throats. Max turned me around and pushed his tongue into my mouth. His arms wrapped around my back, lifting me off the carpet. My hands gripped his shoulders as my head spun and the room whirled, blue curtains and white walls and a messy bed lurching toward us as we fell onto it in a heap.

Max was above me, his eyes fierce and focused as he dived in for the kiss. His lips found my cheek and my ear and my collarbone, traveling down my skin as he pulled up my top then yanked down my bra. There were my breasts, in the middle of Max Morgan's bedroom, pale and pointy, and Max was gawping. And then he was touching. Soft at first, then harder and harder, and he knew what he was doing all right and it felt good so I groaned. I closed my eyes as Max's lips found my nipple and Mr. Harris that's probably where I should leave it tonight because I've got school in the morning, and besides, I'm blushing like anything.

Believe it or not the spider's still here, staring out the shed window at all the black and silver, and if you ask me she must be sleeping because amazing as the universe is, I don't think anyone can look at it for that long without getting bored unless they're Stephen Hawking. I wonder if you can see the sky from your cell and if you ever think about the galaxy and how we're just tiny specks in all this infinity. Sometimes I try to picture my house in the suburbs on the edge of the city, and then I zoom out to see the country, and then I zoom out to see the whole world, and then I zoom out to see the entire universe. There are fiery suns and deep black holes and shooting stars, and I fade into nothing and the trouble that I caused is just a microscopic blip among the mighty cosmic explosions.

There was a mighty cosmic explosion in Mum's car after Max's party. Somehow I made it outside for eleven. I was sobering up fast, but there was no disguising the smell. Of course, it all kicked off as soon as Mum caught a whiff of alcohol. I can't remember what she said, but there was loud stuff about disappointment and angry stuff about trust, and she yelled all the way home as my head started to bang. Dad joined in when I got back in the house, but when I was sent to bed, I shoved my head under the pillow and grinned.

The Boy with the Brown Eyes. Who on earth was he and where had he gone and would I ever see him again? And Max. What would happen when we saw each other at school, and would he kiss me, most probably behind the recycle bin, where no teachers could see? Turning onto my back, I marveled at having two boys who might be interested when a few hours before I'd had none, and as I drifted off to sleep, I found myself thanking Grandpa. I only went to the party because of his stroke, and Mr. Harris even though I was in trouble and most probably grounded for the rest of my life, I couldn't help but think of it as a stroke of good luck.

From,
Zoe
1 Fiction Road
Bath, UK

S. Harris #993765
Polunsky Unit (Death Row)
Livingston, TEXAS 77351
USA
September 17

Dear Mr. Harris,

For once my legs aren't digging into the tiles because I picked up my pillow before I tiptoed out of the house. I put it on top of the box and it's quite comfy even though it's a bit damp. I must have been sweating in my dream and it was so real, with the rain and the trees and the disappearing hand. I bet you're no stranger to this so I don't need to bang on about how terrifying it was. Probably you have nightmares all the time, like when the guard turns off the light I bet you zoom right back to the moment your wife told you the truth.

Funny to think it wasn't your wife who got you the death penalty. I didn't understand that at first. No offense or anything, but stabbing a woman you've been married to for ten years sounds a whole lot worse than shooting a random neighbor who'd popped around with a mincemeat tart because it was Christmas. But then the article, which FYI I found on Google, said something about a crime of passion. When you attacked your wife, you weren't thinking straight. You were blinded by rage and seeing so much red I bet your wife was practically scarlet, which would have been appropriate. That's what you call a woman who's had an affair. A scarlet woman.

In a court of American law, acting out of anger is not as bad as killing in cold blood. When you didn't answer the door the next morning, your neighbor opened it up and strolled into your house. If you ask me, that's bad manners, but I suppose your neighbor learned her lesson when the bullet blew out her brain. Shooting a potential witness was calculating. According to the jury, you knew exactly what you were doing when you pulled the trigger and fed her tart to your dog. You went on the run for three days, but I'm guessing the guilt got too much because you turned yourself in.

Sometimes I think I'd be better off doing that. It's getting harder to pretend now that I'm back at school. Now his mum's sniffing around, too. There I was in English the other day with my phone in my hand, and before you say it, I know I shouldn't have been looking, but I was checking the time, willing it to be lunch so I could escape with Lauren. We've developed this routine where we grab sandwiches then hide away in the music block in this room full of brass instruments where no one can stare. She sits on the case of a trumpet and I lean back against the wall with my feet on a trombone, and we don't say a lot, just complain about the soggy cucumber or the hard tomatoes or the rubbery chicken.

There were five minutes of English left when the time disappeared and a name replaced it on the screen.

SANDRA SANDRA SANDRA

My phone clattered onto the desk, bounced twice, then skidded toward my pencil case.

SANDRA SANDRA SANDRA

"Everything okay, Zoe?"

I jumped. Mrs. Macklin was twisting around from the board. I couldn't even nod. A boy with freckles started to laugh.

"Shut it, Paul!" Lauren shouted from the other side of the classroom because we were sitting in alphabetical order and, Mr. Harris, I don't think it's giving too much away to say her last name begins with a *W* whereas mine begins with a *J*. The boy closed his mouth but kept smirking. Other people were smiling, too, nudging each other and pointing in my direction.

"What's the matter, Zoe?" Mrs. Macklin asked, peering over the top of her glasses, her eyes full of concern.

"I'm fine," I managed.

SANDRA SANDRA SANDRA SANDR—

She hung up but left a message. When the bell rang, I disappeared into the girls' toilets before Lauren could ask what was wrong. Heart pounding, I collapsed on the toilet, pictures spinning through my mind—police and prisons and orange jumpsuits and courts and newspaper headlines screaming GUILTY! Sandra had realized the truth about May 1, I was sure of it. Panic started at my fingertips and crawled up my arms into my chest and right up to my scalp, pulling at the roots of my hair.

"Anyone in there?" someone asked, banging on the stall door.

"Yeah," I called, holding my phone with trembling fingers.

"Hurry up, then," the girl said, and I nodded even though she couldn't see me then pressed the button to play the message before I could change my mind.

There was a pause. A long one. I closed my eyes. Sandra's voice came at last and it was quiet and croaky and full of these hesitations that made the sentences sound broken. She asked me to pay her a visit sometime. I opened one eye. She thought it would be nice for both of us. I opened the other. She told me that not a day goes by when she doesn't wonder how I'm doing, and just before she hung up, she said it would mean a lot if I could pop in every now and again.

"No one else really . . . understands, do they? People . . . well, they don't have a clue."

It goes without saying that I didn't call her back and I deleted the message, shoving the phone into my bag as far as it would go, burying it under thousands of years in my History textbook. When I found Lauren in the music room, she handed me a

41

sandwich and studied my face, but she didn't ask me why I couldn't eat it, just commented that the chicken was even more rubbery than usual.

From,
Zoe
1 Fiction Road
Bath, UK

S. Harris #993765
Polunsky Unit (Death Row)
Livingston, Texas 77351
USA

October 27

Dear Mr. Harris,

Sorry it's been so long but I've been struggling quite a lot recently, and I even messed up the test on plant reproduction. Not to boast but I probably would have got an A if Dad hadn't come into my room the night I was supposed to be revising.

He told me he'd bumped into Sandra at the supermarket in the vegetable aisle and her eyes had filled with tears that had nothing to do with onions.

"She'd love to see you," Dad had said as I stared at my Biology textbook, willing him to shut up. "Mentioned she'd called you a couple of times but you hadn't answered."

"Shouldn't phone me at school, then," I mumbled, and then I

felt bad. None of this was Sandra's fault. I dug the end of my pen into a diagram of a flower, desperate for Dad to leave.

"She looked dreadful," Dad went on, sitting on the edge of my bed. "Really awful." I winced, the guilt actually painful. "Lost a ton of weight. Practically skin and bone."

"All right! I get it!" I snapped, flinging my pen onto the carpet.

Dad fiddled with the edge of the duvet. "Just thought you might like to know you're not on your own, pet. That's all. I shouldn't have said anything." Dad stood up heavily and rubbed the top of my head. "If I could feel it for you, I would," he murmured, and honest truth I would have given anything to push my pain right into his chest, which was a horrible thing to want to do so I started to cry. I didn't deserve a nice family or friends or even someone like you and that's why I've not written for a while.

But tonight I realized you might be lonely in your cell without my letters. No offense or anything but I can't imagine you have many friends on Death Row, like I'm sure it's not the most sociable of places with everyone telling jokes and doing high fives through the cell bars. Maybe you've come to rely on me as much as I rely on you. Perhaps we need each other so I shouldn't feel too bad about telling you my story, which I desperately need to do because it's eating me up inside and you're the only person in the world who might understand. I can't wait a second longer so I'll start the morning after Max's party with me lying in bed suffering from my first-ever hangover, probably making this noise: *ajooodfeeoihfiidjog*.

*   *   *

Surprise surprise, Mum didn't care that I was more ill than ever in my life. She yanked my curtains apart. Sunshine punched me between the eyes with a bright yellow fist.

"Up," she ordered, opening my window, which looked out over the back garden. "Shower. Breakfast. Dusting."

"Dusting?" I croaked.

"And then vacuuming. And you can clean the bathroom as well." I pulled the duvet over my head. Mum pulled it back again. "*Drinking*, Zoe. What were you thinking?"

"I didn't mean to do it. I didn't even drink that much."

"Drinking anything at your age is unacceptable. Completely unacceptable. This is a big year for you, Zoe. Start of your GCSEs. Coursework. You know your father and I have high hopes for you. There's no point frowning," she said, because I'd pulled a face. I hated the school conversation. "You may be bright, but if you want to go into law, you're going to have to get the top grades." I glanced at *Bizzle the Bazzlebog* on my desk. "Writing silly children's stories doesn't pay," Mum said firmly. "Law does. We've talked about this. You agree with me."

"I know," I muttered, though it wasn't true. It was the same whenever careers were mentioned. It was easier to go along with whatever Mum said because I felt as if I owed her for all the hard work she was putting in.

"Well, then. You're going to have to work hard. Not throw your chances down the drain."

"It was only a couple of drinks, Mum. I won't do it again."

45

"You won't have the chance to do it again," she said, picking my jeans off the carpet and hanging them in the closet. "You're grounded for two months. And I'm taking your phone."

I didn't move for an hour. I actually couldn't. Even lifting my head to have a drink of water made me feel sick. Dad told Dot I had the flu so she sprinted into my bedroom in her pajamas, holding out a blue cardboard crown. She'd written GET WELL SOON on the front, except she'd forgotten one of the o's so it said GET WELL SON. On top of her own head was a bigger crown made out of pink cardboard. She beamed when I put mine on.

"Now we can be the King and Queen of the World and also the Universe," she signed.

I bowed and held up the duvet. "Climb in, Your Majesty." Dot scrambled into my bed, and we cuddled for ages, the spikes of our crowns jutting out on the pillow.

I did my chores eventually, dragging myself around the house in my bathrobe. As I scrubbed the bathroom, my mind jumped between the two boys so I drew two hearts in the toilet bowl with yellow bleach.

yellow bleach

When I flushed, it made the water frothy, which just so happened to be exactly how I felt, my excitement bubbling all over itself. I couldn't wait to tell Lauren, picturing her face as I described the kiss with Max. Maybe I'd see him at lunch. The Boy with the Brown Eyes, too. We'd share secret smiles over fish and chips, the tang of salt and vinegar and love in our noses.

All things considered, I was in a pretty good mood. Mum and Dad barely spoke to me, but they didn't say much to each other, either, no doubt still seething from the night before. Dad was in the garage, polishing the BMW, and Mum was busy with Dot, practicing the lip-reading that the speech therapist set as homework.

"Bank," Mum said clearly. "Bank. Bank. Bank."

"Pant?" Dot signed.

Soph pulled a face. Dressed head to foot in black, she was lying on the living room floor with her white rabbit, Skull. A math book lay at her side. Dot was sitting on Mum's lap in a leather armchair, her eyebrows scrunched up underneath her pink crown.

"Nearly," Mum said, but a line appeared in the middle of her forehead.

"Can we stop now?" Dot signed, scratching the end of her nose and looking fed up.

"I'm stuck on question four," Soph announced, but Mum adjusted the crown on Dot's head and carried on.

Soph picked up her math book and held it in the air, the stone of her mood ring glinting dark blue.

"Find the mean average of the following numbers. How can an average be *mean*? It doesn't make—"

47

"Back," Mum interrupted. Dot sucked on her bottom lip, thinking. "Back," Mum said again. She pointed over her shoulder to give Dot a clue. *"Back."*

"Back?" Dot signed, and Mum actually cheered.

"Good girl!" she said, shaking Dot's arms in celebration. Dot giggled as Mum pecked her on the cheek. Soph tossed her math book onto the carpet.

"Pen?" she muttered, and I nodded.

A few minutes later, Soph held out a red one. We were crouching among Mum's shoes in the big closet in my parents' bedroom, where we always smoked pens and discussed stuff that needed darkness. Soph put a blue pen in her mouth and pretended to inhale. She blew out nothing and tapped the pen three times into Mum's sneaker as if getting rid of ash. I sucked on my pen and exhaled slowly.

"How was the party?" Soph asked. "You were so drunk, Zo. When you came in, you did this hiccup that made you sound like a seal."

I nudged her with my toe as she did a loud impression. "Shut up!"

Soph grinned, putting her chin on her knees, her long hair falling around her legs. "What was it like, then?"

"What was what like?"

"Being drunk," she whispered, her eyes shining in the darkness.

I thought for a moment. "Dizzy."

"Dizzy good or dizzy bad?"

"Dizzy medium. It started off quite fun, but then I felt awful."

"What did you drink?"

"Vodka and this whiskey a boy gave me."

"A *boy*. Did you kiss him?"

"Of course," I said, taking a long, sophisticated drag of my pen.

"Who was it?"

"Someone called Max."

"Good-looking?"

"Very. And he's popular and practically everyone in the school likes him."

"So why did he kiss *you*, then?" she smirked.

I kicked her again but decided to be honest. "I don't know. He was really drunk." Something inside me twisted but I kept my voice casual. "He probably won't even remember tomorrow. You know what boys are like."

She dropped her pen in Mum's sneaker and started fiddling with the laces. "Sounds better than listening to Mum and Dad arguing, anyway."

"Grandpa?"

Soph nodded, tying a big bow. "Is he going to die, Zo?"

"At some point."

"You know what I mean."

"He's old," I replied because I didn't know what else to say.

Soph lifted the sneaker by the loop of the bow and tapped the base of the shoe. It swung from side to side like a pendulum.

"I reckon he should come and live with us," she said. "I don't think he should be on his own if he's dying."

"We don't have any spare rooms."

"I could move in with you," Soph suggested.

"No chance! You snore like a pig."

"Don't."

"Do. Anyway, Mum would never let him in the house."

The sneaker moved back and forward in the air.

"Why not?" Soph asked.

I put the pen in my mouth and sucked, trying to remember the argument at Grandpa's house all those years before. Before I could answer, Mum shouted up the stairs. Soph tapped the sneaker a bit harder. It swung more violently.

"Soph!" Mum called again. I nudged my sister, but she didn't move. "*Soph! Piano.*"

"Now she's got time," she muttered, letting the sneaker fly off her finger, sending it crashing against the wooden door.

We were just about to climb out of the closet when Mum entered the bedroom and took off her slippers, placing them neatly by the bed. Massaging her forehead, she sank onto the mattress. Dad followed, pulling off his oily shirt and dropping it on the carpet.

"Laundry basket," Mum said.

"Give me a second," Dad snapped, taking his trousers off, too.

Soph's hand slammed over her mouth, hiding a tiny snort of laughter. The lid of the laundry basket was lifted. There was a *flump* as clothes were thrown inside. I bent forward slowly to get a better view through the crack.

"I've been thinking," Dad started.

"Not now, Simon." Mum plumped up the cream pillow then settled back onto it. "My head's pounding."

"Just hear me out, okay?"

Mum frowned but said, "Go on."

"Why don't we compromise on Zoe?"

Soph dug her fingers into my leg, and I shrugged in the darkness.

"What do you mean?" Mum asked.

"Well, if you think Soph and Dot are too young to visit my dad, Zoe can still go."

"I don't want any of the girls to visit him," Mum replied. "It's the principle of the matter."

Dad sat down on the bed. "Principles are hardly important anymore."

"How can you say that?"

"You didn't see him, Jane. He was old. Lonely. We've ignored him for years, and I—"

"He's ignored us, too! And we would never have severed ties if he hadn't said . . . if he hadn't accused . . . It was *unforgivable*. You've said so yourself a hundred times! And now you're expecting me to forget about it and play happy family? No," she said resolutely. "I can't do that."

Dad looked as if he was about to argue but stood up instead. For a few minutes, neither of them spoke as Dad put on some clean clothes.

"How was the lip-reading?" he asked at last. "Any better?" The pillow rustled as Mum shook her head from side to side, looking worried. Dad didn't seem to notice. He pulled on a sock

51

then tugged it off again, examining it closely. "Hole. Are there any clean ones on the radiator?" When Mum didn't reply, he said, "Don't stress, pet. She'll get there."

"You don't know that."

"'Course I do. If you keep practicing."

"Practicing might not be enough," Mum replied, propping herself up on her elbows. "I've been thinking about it. A lot, actually."

"I know what you're going to say," Dad muttered as he threw the holey sock back into his drawer. "And the answer's no."

"But why? What's wrong with trying surgery again?"

"We're not putting her through it," Dad said, referring to the cochlear implant that had gotten infected and had to be removed. "Dot's happy as she is."

"But surgery might help!"

"She can make that decision for herself when she's older."

"It might be too late when she's older," Mum argued, flopping onto her back.

Dad gazed down at her. "You worry too much."

He leaned forward to kiss the deep line in the middle of Mum's forehead. And then her nose. And then her lips. Soph grabbed my leg, her face screwed up in disgust, but she needn't have worried, because Mum rolled away from Dad to face the wall.

I stared at my own wall that night, too excited to sleep. Next day, I jumped out of bed before even my alarm, and Mr. Harris I bet you know how it feels to get ready with trembling fingers. According to the article I found on Google, for your first date you took Alice for a cheeseburger with curly fries, and you probably did something romantic, e.g., drank chocolate milk shake out of one glass with two straws. The journalist said you met her when you were eighteen at a baseball game because you were the bowler and she was a cheerleader, and it was true love for ten years until you stabbed her.

When I arrived at school, Lauren spotted me by the art department and came running over. For once in my life, I had a story to tell, and I almost laughed out loud as she grabbed my arm and yanked me into an empty classroom. Pictures hung from pegs above our heads and the windowsill was crammed full of jars holding paintbrushes.

"You heard about Max, then?" I said, grinning. "I wanted to tell you yesterday, but Mum took my phone and made me dust. And clean the toilet. *Toilets*, actually. The one in the main bathroom was disgusting."

"So that's why you didn't answer! I've been calling you and calling you. Left you about a hundred messages."

She sounded stressed. Looked it, too, tucking her black hair behind her ears, where it didn't stay because it was too short.

"What's up?" I asked slowly.

"You're not going to like this." She pulled her phone out of her pocket and stared at the screen, picking her lip with her finger. "Max sent the picture to Jack," she whispered. "And Jack sent it to everyone else. *Everyone*."

As Lauren turned the screen toward me, I sank onto a stool, my stomach falling into my shoes.

A picture.

A picture of me with my eyes closed, my hair fanned out on

the duvet, completely topless, apart from a flimsy red bra that didn't leave much to the imagination. As I groaned, Lauren rubbed my shoulder.

"At least you've got good tits."

Really good ones, apparently. Every time I walked into a classroom, someone wolf-whistled, and boys I didn't know stared at me in the corridors, and this tall guy stopped me by the PE department after lunch.

"Where've you been hiding?" he said in a creepy voice as I shuddered.

I hadn't been hiding anywhere. I'd been in the same classrooms at the same school for three entire years. Writing stuff down in my books. Listening to the teacher. Talking to Lauren on the playground. But all of a sudden, people were gazing at me in class and studying me in locker rooms and watching me buy a cheese sandwich from the cafeteria as if I was doing something different. Something interesting.

I'd wanted attention, but not like this. It was a relief when the final bell rang. Gray clouds had gathered in the sky, and it was cold so I buried my face in my coat and hurried past the basketball courts. Max appeared at the school gate a few meters in front of me. He was tossing a soccer ball into the air, his bag at his feet, and his short dark hair was carefully styled, sort of sticking up at the front. He looked good, no doubt about it, but that was irrelevant. Completely irrelevant. I told myself so again and again as my chest started to flutter.

A group of girls slowed down to watch as I focused on the exit, marching past Max, my nose most probably in the air.

"Zoe! Wait!"

I spun around so fast I got a mouthful of my own hair. I swiped it out of my face. Max dropped the ball, surprised I was angry.

"When did you take it?" I asked, charging toward him. The group of girls gawped, five mouths opening at the exact same moment. Max shifted about on the spot. "I don't remember you having a phone."

"Everyone's got a phone," he said lamely. "And I told you I was taking a picture. Relax." He chanced a smile. "It's not a big deal. No different from being in a bikini, if you think about it. Nothing to get upset about."

"Don't patronize me," I growled. "And don't lie. You didn't say *anything* about taking a picture."

Smirking, he leaned in close, smelling of aftershave and chewing gum.

"'Course I did. You just don't remember. It's not my fault you can't take your alcohol." He actually winked. "Honestly, you were so drunk. . . ."

"Everyone's seen it," I said, my voice shaking with fury. "The whole school. How dare you? I mean, what gives you the right? Just because you're popular? Is that it? You think you can do whatever you like?"

Max blew out his cheeks. "No. Don't be stupid."

"Oh, I'm not the stupid one. You are. You thought you could flirt your way out of it like I'm some dumb girl who's going to be appeased by a wink from the Mighty Max Morgan." I looked him up and down in disgust. *"Please."*

He whispered, "You're so cute when you're angry." Snarling in frustration, I made to leave, but Max grabbed my hand. "Look, it wasn't my fault, all right?" I tried to protest, but he carried on quickly. "Well, it wasn't. I only sent the photo to Jack. He was the one who forwarded——"

"But you were the one who took it in the first place!" I spat. "*Without* me knowing!"

Rain was falling now, heavy drops of water splattering my coat.

"I'm sorry, okay? I'll make it up to you."

I snatched my hand away. "How, exactly?"

Max's face softened for a moment. He was about to speak when three of his friends sprinted toward the bike shed, shirts sticking to their skin.

"Asking for another photo?" Jack yelled, unlocking his bike.

Max held up his hands as if he'd been caught out. "Guilty!"

"Don't blame you, mate. She looked good."

"Well." Max shrugged, all his cockiness back in a flash. "Not bad."

He winked once more before running off, and Mr. Harris I think that's where I'll stop tonight, with Max jumping onto the back of Jack's bike and speeding out of the school gate with his head thrown back in laughter. Next time I'll tell you what happened at the bonfire, and believe me you'll be shocked, but don't worry, you won't have to wait ages for the next part of the story. It's been such a relief to talk to you again, and maybe you got something out of it, too. Honest truth, my heart aches for you trapped in prison with no distraction to speak of. All I can hope is that I'm wrong about Death Row and there's a friendly inmate in the cell next to yours. I'm crossing my fingers he's a chatty rapist who knows a few good jokes as well.

From,
Zoe
1 Fiction Road
Bath, UK

S. HARRIS #993765

POLUNSKY UNIT (DEATH ROW)

LIVINGSTON, TEXAS 77351

USA

November 3

Hello again, Mr. Harris,

The clocks have changed so it's getting darker an hour earlier, not that it makes much difference to us because the world's always black when we talk. I wonder if your meal arrived when the stars were brighter and the moon shone earlier because the guards had put back the clocks. Now I come to think of it, I bet they didn't even bother. I bet it doesn't matter to criminals if it's 3 PM or 5 PM or 7 PM. Probably it doesn't even matter that it's a Sunday. If every hour of every day is the same, I guess time just disappears.

Time didn't disappear when I was grounded after Max's party last year. September was slow, but October barely moved.

After the excitement with the photo, school went back to normal, and in case you're wondering, I never got to see the back of the recycle bin. I didn't bump into The Boy with the Brown Eyes, either, and life plodded on for a few weeks with nothing much happening except a lot of bickering from Mum and Dad because he kept coming home late after visiting Grandpa at the hospital. At first Mum would plate up his dinner and leave it in the microwave, but then one evening she chucked it in the trash, and Mr. Harris I reckon that's a good place for us to begin tonight.

"There's a can of beans in the cupboard," Mum said when Dad stared inside the empty microwave, his hands on his hips. He sniffed the air, and I wondered if he could smell the chili con carne we'd eaten earlier and the beef Soph had spilled on the carpet when she'd tried to smuggle a bit to Skull.

Dad got a can opener out of the drawer. "Grandpa's no better," he sighed. Mum made no sign that she'd heard him, gazing closely at the laptop screen. Dad poured the beans into a bowl, and I imagined Bizzle plopping out all blue and wet and covered in sauce. I smiled to myself, keen to finish my homework so I could write another chapter of the story. "Good day, then, folks?"

"Average," Mum muttered.

"Probably better than mine."

"It's not a competition, Simon."

"Didn't say it was. I've just had a right stinker, that's all. I need to talk to you about it, actually." He punched some buttons on the microwave, then watched the bowl rotate slowly.

"I'm a little busy at the moment," Mum said.

"It's important."

"So is this."

"What are you looking at?"

"Nothing that would interest you," she sniffed.

"If that's what I think it is, you're wasting your time."

"No harm in looking," Mum said, clicking on a page about cochlear implants as the microwave *ping*ed. Dad pulled out the bowl and stuck his finger into the beans.

"How long do you put these in for? They're still cold."

"Oh, for heaven's sake," Mum snapped, standing up and making a grab for the bowl. Dad didn't let go of the other side. "Can't you do anything for yourself?"

"I didn't say you had to do it!"

Mum yanked the bowl out of Dad's hands and flung it back inside the microwave.

"Give us a second, Zo," Dad said in a low voice. "I need to talk to your mother."

"I'm working," I muttered, not looking up from my homework. I tapped a pen between my teeth to show I was thinking hard and not to be disturbed.

"Just five minutes, pet. Please?"

"Leave her, Simon. She's studying."

"She can study in her bedroom," Dad replied. "Go on, Zo."

In a huff, I picked up my books and disappeared out of the kitchen. Of course, I did what any normal person would do and put a glass against the living room wall, but all I could hear was the blood swirling around my own brain. They were in there for an hour. The next three nights, too. I had no idea what they were talking about, and when Soph stuck a straw underneath the gap in the door to spy, all she could see was a bit of fluff on the carpet.

A week later, things got even stranger. I came back from school to find Dad pacing up and down the hall, loosening his tie. Mum's bum was sticking out of the shoe closet.

"Where're you going?" I asked, my stomach clenching. Dad never came home early.

"Out," Mum said, shoving her feet into a pair of high heels.

"Well, obviously. But where? To see Grandpa?"

"Not likely," Mum replied, dropping her bag on the hall table next to a pamphlet about Bonfire Night. She put on some lipstick as Dad bobbed up and down on the balls of his feet.

"Why are you all dressed up?" I asked.

"You don't need to worry about that," Dad said.

I took off my coat and put it on the banister. "But I am worried about it."

Mum rubbed her lips together and fiddled with the collar of her blouse. "We'll explain later. Soph's on the computer, and Dot's playing with her dolls. I've made some pasta so you can have that if you get hungry." She paused, looking worried. "Promise you'll watch your sisters and call me if anything—"

"If I do that, can I go to this tomorrow night?" I interrupted, holding up the pamphlet about the bonfire. Mum read the details. "It's been two months," I reminded her. "Everyone at school's going, and I was only meant to be grounded for—"

"All right," Mum replied, picking up the keys to the BMW. "But only if you get your homework done. And fix your tie, Simon."

Dad ignored her, snatching the keys from her hand as he closed the front door.

Mr. Harris, I was convinced they were going to see a lawyer about getting a divorce. I sank onto the stairs, feeling sick. I knew exactly how it was going to be. I'd heard about it from people at school. Dad would rent a flat and eat fish sticks every night and forget to buy washing-up liquid so there wouldn't be enough clean knives and we'd have to spread butter with the back of a spoon. Mum would put on forty pounds and lie on the sofa in pajamas, watching documentaries about women who used to be men. That was precisely what happened to Lauren's mum until Lauren said enough is enough and turned off the TV just as Bob's new breasts were about to be revealed. Her mum was annoyed, but it was a wake-up call, and she lost weight by only eating protein then went on a date in a pair of Lauren's size-eight jeans.

I stared at my own jeans drying on the radiator. I couldn't let it happen to my family. I crept into my parents' bedroom and started going through Mum's bedside table to find out what was going on. In the top drawer was a jewelry box with a key in the lock. Checking the coast was clear, I turned it, hearing a satisfying *click*. Inside were bits of baby hair in little plastic bags from me and Soph, tiny prints of our hands and feet, and the wristbands we wore in the hospital when we were born. Dot's baby stuff must've been in another box, but I didn't try to look for it because my attention had been caught by a letter in a yellowing envelope underneath a bag containing my first baby tooth.

Dad's handwriting, but faded. I can't remember exactly what it said, but there was cheesy stuff about Mum's blond hair feeling like gold silk and her green eyes looking like calm rock pools and her confidence shining like starlight, powerful and sparkling and lighting up all the darkness around her. The mum I knew was worried about parabens and putting red socks in the wash with white T-shirts and making sure we took our vitamins. I felt sort of sad that I never knew this other woman, but I put everything back in the correct place then opened a second drawer.

A whole load of stuff about cochlear implants, printed off the Internet, pages and pages of it, highlighted in pink. Underneath that was a letter from the bank saying something about a remortgage. *Remortgage.* I'd never heard of the word, but the letter looked official. Feeling as if I was getting somewhere, I forced myself onto Soph's lap in the study.

"Get off!" she cried. I sat down harder, taking over the computer. "Oh God, Zo, you're so heavy!"

I found this forum for middle-aged people. TeaCozy7 said she was considering it to pay for a patio. Considering what, though? I searched further. Remortgaging turned out to be a way of releasing money tied up in a house if you wanted funds to buy something big, or if you were having money troubles.

"Money troubles?" Soph asked, peering around my body. "Who's having money troubles?"

"We are," I said happily. Well, it was better than divorce.

We got hungry before my parents came home so I heated up the pasta, and we ate it at the kitchen table. When Soph was picking at the bits of olive left on her plate, I stole her phone and sprinted upstairs as she swiped at my heels. Charging into the bathroom, I turned the lock and called Lauren. Soph posted a note under the door saying that I was DEAD in block capitals next to a picture of me with a knife stabbing my brain and a PS that asked if she could borrow a protractor to finish her math homework. Mum and Dad came back while I was chatting in the empty bath, my feet propped up on the gold taps.

"Get down here, Zoe!" Mum shouted.

"So, promise I can come and live with you if we're made homeless?" I asked Lauren.

"Sure. We'll start our own business, like a dog-walking business called The Dog's Bollocks because we'll be the best at what we do."

"*Zoe!*" Mum called again.

"I have to go. See you at the bonfire tomorrow," I said quickly.

"Give me a bark."

"I have to go!"

"Only if you bark."

"Woof."

Lauren laughed as I ended the call. On the landing, there was a flash of silver as a shiny figure hurtled toward me.

"What are you doing?" I gasped. Dot was dressed head to foot in tinsel.

"I found the Christmas decorations in Mum and Dad's room."

I dropped to my knees and signed quickly. "You have to take it off! I was supposed to be looking after you!"

Dot spun on the spot with her arms in the air. "I can't wait for Christmas," she signed. "For Santa. Is it true he brings you anything you want?"

"Yes," I said. "But you have to—"

"*Anything* in the whole wide world?" she signed, watching me closely.

"*Yes.* But you have to change."

Dot pointed at two baubles dangling from her ears. "Do you like my jewelry?"

I gritted my teeth. "I love it. But please go and take it all off. Mum's home."

Dot's eyes widened, and she shot off, running into her room and slamming the door. In the kitchen, I found Mum piling up the dirty plates by the sink.

"Thought you'd leave the washing up for me?"

I rolled up my sleeves. "Sorry."

"And have you made a start on your homework?"

"Not yet."

"Zoe!"

"I've got all weekend!" I protested, filling the sink with water. "And I've only got to answer a few math questions and write an introduction for my English essay."

"Essay? You didn't mention that!"

"It's only the opening paragraph."

"Still, you can't rush it."

"I didn't say I was going to *rush* it," I muttered, scrubbing tomato and garlic sauce off a plate. "I know what I'm doing."

"I'll help you."

"You don't need to, Mum. I've got all these notes from my teacher. Practically a whole notebook full of them."

Mum opened the fridge looking for something to eat as I put the clean plate on the draining board. "Well, I'll check it for you when you're done. English is important for law."

"English is important for writing, too," I said, too quietly for her to hear.

She took some salad out of the fridge and pressed a tomato between her fingers to check it was ripe. "This'll do. Not very hungry, to be honest."

"Are you and Dad buying a patio?" I asked suddenly.

"A patio? No. Why do you ask?"

I started on another plate. "No reason."

The following day was the bonfire, and Mr. Harris I might be wrong, but I don't think you celebrate Bonfire Night in America so I will explain all about it right now. Four centuries ago, November 5, 1605, to be precise, Guy Fawkes and his friends tried to blow up the Houses of Parliament to kill the king. It was Guy Fawkes's job to set off the gunpowder in the cellar, but the murder attempt failed, and everyone was so relieved that they lit fires and had parties to celebrate. The ritual stuck. People have been doing it in England ever since. On November 5, everyone makes a model of Guy Fawkes out of old clothes stuffed with newspapers, e.g., *The Sun* (or *The Times*, if you want his limbs to be a bit posher), then they toss him into the flames. If you ask me, it's a bit harsh, people eating toffee apples as Guy Fawkes burns to death for a crime he didn't even commit, but the night is still fun, with fireworks and sparklers and smoke that stays in your hair for days.

The local one was at a park just outside the city center so imagine open green spaces and bike trails and footpaths and woods and a surging river. The entrance was marked by a large iron gate, and when Dad dropped me off, the air smelled of freedom. Okay, and also hot dogs and smoke and cotton candy, if you want me to be accurate about it, but freedom more than anything else.

The fire burned in the middle of the park, orange and red and shimmering yellow. Crowds migrated toward it, moths to a flame, and I was one of them, stretching my wings for the first time in weeks. Lauren was sitting on a bench, so I did that thing of sneaking up behind her, jabbing her sides, and shouting "boo" as she swore—*FFFFFFFFFFFFFFFFFFFF!*—just like that, at the top of her voice. The word echoed in all the empty space because there was so much of it, a whole universe, in fact, ready to be explored. I plunked down next to her and we chatted for ages, eating cotton candy as the fire turned the night golden.

All the sugar made me thirsty so I left Lauren to guard the bench and went in search of water. Women selling T-shirts and others selling jewelry and men flogging toys spread out in stalls along the bank of the river. Water gushed and smoke swirled and vendors called out as I looked for a drinks stand. A man with a beard held out a model of a red Ferrari, a.k.a. Dad's dream car, so I stopped and bought it because he'd been worried about Grandpa.

Handing over some money, I saw The Boy with the Brown Eyes by the glowing edge of the fire. By the way, I know full well I could have built up the tension here, especially as we've learned how to do that in English using short sentences and pauses and hints to create suspense. The problem Mr. Harris is this is real life, not fiction, so I wanted to reflect how it actually happened. In real life, things don't build up nicely to a climax. In actual fact, moments occur out of the blue and there's no warning, like the time Dad hit a dog.

In a book, no doubt there would have a couple of near misses to foreshadow the event, and maybe even a bark as Dad sped around the corner to hint to the reader that something bad was about to take place. In real life, Dad was driving back from the supermarket and the sun was shining and "Dancing Queen" came on the radio as he went over a speed bump that turned out to be a Labrador. And that's how it happened at the bonfire. No buildup. No warning. One second I was turning away from the stall, and the next I was facing him, The Boy with the Brown Eyes. Just like that.

"Your car."

"What?"

The man held out the Ferrari. "Your car."

I shoved it into my front pocket, never taking my eyes off the boy. He was wearing a T-shirt with white writing on the front, staring into the flames and daydreaming about something no doubt important. I pictured a thought cloud above his brain and me diving headfirst right into the middle of it. I forgot about being thirsty. I forgot about Lauren. Pulse racing, I hurried toward the fire, pushing to the front, squeezing past a dad with a little girl on his shoulders and a woman with a poodle in one of those tartan overcoats.

Sparks flew, burning bits of amber turning black above the flames.

"Shall I throw him in?" someone shouted. The crowd cheered. A man held up a model of Guy Fawkes wearing a Halloween mask. His legs were stuffed in green trousers, and his arms jutted out of a cardigan. "Shall I throw him in?" the man shouted more loudly. The little girl clapped her hands. Even the poodle wagged its tail.

The Boy with the Brown Eyes yawned and looked away. I shuffled forward to make my presence more obvious as the man grabbed Guy Fawkes by an arm and a leg. He swung the dummy toward the fire. The head skimmed the flames, and I winced as the crowd roared.

"One..." Necks strained to get a better look. "Two..." Everyone joined in the count. *"Three!"*

The fire spat. Guy Fawkes flew. And just as the dummy

disappeared into the blaze, the boy turned away from the crowd and looked straight at me.

The words on his T-shirt said SAVE GUY FAWKES. For five seconds, we stared at each other, and then the boy smiled.

"Hi." That one word sent me soaring. The bonfire vanished. The people, too. There was just me and the boy and our eyes shining at the center of the universe.

"Nice top," I said at last. "I feel sorry for Guy Fawkes."

"Even though he's a villain?"

"Guy Fawkes had his reasons. Maybe they were good ones."

The boy's eyes twinkled. "Good reasons to do bad things . . . Interesting."

"Very interesting." That cable between our brains burned red. I blushed and looked away. Somewhere a million miles away, the dummy's mask melted.

"Nothing like a good burning to bring people closer together," the boy grinned.

"Maybe we should chuck the poodle in next," I suggested as the dog barked, all fierce fluff in tartan.

The boy laughed. "Maybe it's Scottish. If it's Scottish, I'll let the owners off. What's your name?" he asked suddenly. This time I told him. The two syllables felt new and shiny on my lips. "Better than *Bird Girl*," the boy said, "which is what I've been calling you in my head since the party. Well, that or *Mousetrap*." My heart skipped a beat. It skipped a thousand beats. He'd been thinking of me, too.

"I'm guessing you're not *The Boy with the Brown Eyes*, either."

"That's just my middle name. First name's Aaron."

70

Before I could say anything else, a hand appeared on Aaron's arm.

"Hi!" a girl said. That one word sent me crashing back down to Earth. She had long red hair the color of fire. A black coat the color of coal. A smile for Aaron that burned in my brain long after it had disappeared.

"You're here!" he said, pulling the girl into a hug. She peered over his shoulder—pale skin with the perfect amount of freckles and a straight nose a plastic surgeon would have been proud of.

"I really need to talk to you," she whispered in his ear, her fingers on the back of his neck.

"Sure," he said, which was the exact opposite of the response I wanted him to give, but I tried my best to smile with that French word *nonchalance* as he apologized to me and stepped closer to the heat for a private conversation.

I glanced at my watch. Quarter past nine. Forty-five minutes until Mum picked me up.

Forty-four minutes.

Forty-three minu—

"There you are! I thought you'd been murdered or something." Lauren appeared at my side, looking grumpy. "Where've you been?"

Holding out my hands to the fire, I pretended to shiver. "Just cold."

"You could've told me. I'm bloody freezing. And about to die of thirst so I had to give up the bench. I put my bag on it, but this old guy hobbled up to me and was like 'You can't reserve this seat' and started going on about his wife needing to rest."

"That's quite sweet."

"That's quite *mental*. He was on his own so I reckon he's one of those people who see things that aren't there. You know, like necrophilia or whatever."

I hid a smile. "You mean schizophrenia."

"What?"

"Schizophrenia. Necrophilia is, well, you don't want to know."

I stared at Aaron's back. Forty-one minutes until Mum arrived.

Lauren shook my arm. "Come on, then."

"Come on what?"

She jiggled on the spot. "I'm thirsty."

Aaron was holding the girl's hands between his, his eyes glued to her face.

"Yeah, okay," I said, turning away from the fire, feeling cold in a way that had nothing to do with the disappearing flames.

In the line, Lauren was talking nineteen to the dozen, and I'm not entirely sure what that means, but Mr. Harris if you imagine nineteen tongues in her mouth then you'll sort of get the picture. On and on she went about this boy in the year above, one she kissed at Max's party, and I was doing my best to concentrate, but it was difficult when Aaron was putting his arm around the girl in the distance.

Lauren paid for a bottle of water as a firework zoomed into the sky. *Ooohs* from the crowds. *Aaahs*. Without even thinking about it, I grabbed her arm, and we dropped to the ground right there and then to watch the display, lying on the grass as the night exploded all around us. I pointed at some blue sparks.

"They look like tadpoles."

"More like sperm," Lauren said. We both laughed because it was true, the sparks wiggling through the sky as if they were in a race to fertilize the moon. Lauren mimicked the movement with her hand. "Swim, spermies."

A face leaned over us. "Nice."

Blond hair. Brown eyes. Fireworks burst behind his head as my heart erupted in a great flash of red. Aaron.

Lauren put her hand over her eyes. I blinked and looked closer. The boy in the year above held out his hand and pulled Lauren to her feet. I heaved myself off the ground, disappointed.

"I've been looking for you," he said. "Let's go for a walk by the river."

Lauren linked my arm. "Only if Zoe can come, too."

"Don't worry about me," I said, suddenly needing to be alone. More people had joined the fire, but Aaron and the girl had disappeared from view. Lauren examined my expression closely. I made my eyes really big and insistent. "Honestly. I'll be fine. My mum's coming in ten minutes anyway," I lied. The boy tugged Lauren's hand, and she kissed my cheek, making a squeaking noise in my ear.

The flames were roaring now. Smoke made my eyes water and heat stung my skin. I ended up back at the bench to see the old man talking to thin air. It was sad, but only from the outside. I mean, he looked happy enough, telling his invisible wife how fireworks are made, going into great detail about how they're put together to get the different colors. Mr. Harris, I wonder if you ever talk to Alice, and what you say to her if she does appear in your cell, wafting through the bars and hovering near the lightbulb. Maybe you apologize, and I hope she says it's okay, because, after all, it was sort of her fault in the first place.

Families were leaving together and couples were cuddling up by the fire and even the old man had someone to talk to, and who cared if it was in his head rather than real. I trudged to the parking lot and slumped onto a wall. A clock glowed on a church in the distance, and I sighed. After feeling as though I was running out of it, there was now too much left. Twenty minutes with nothing to do except—

Voices!

A boy's. And a girl's.

I shifted along the wall until I was hidden behind a bush and watched Aaron walk into the parking lot, followed by the girl with long red hair. My stomach twisted. They were leaving together, walking easily with their arms around each other's waists. An old blue car with a dented roof and a license plate that said DORIS was parked underneath a streetlight. I peeped through the leaves. Aaron opened the passenger door and kissed the top of the girl's head before she climbed in. My stomach twisted tighter, draining any hope right out of it.

Now, Mr. Harris, you're probably expecting me to kick the bush or burst into tears or run into the parking lot and cause a scene. Well, sorry to disappoint you and all that, but my face was completely calm and my body was completely still. The only thing I did was tear a spiderweb, swiping it in two with the side of my hand. Half of it was left on the wall and half of it dangled from a branch, and that was the only evidence in the whole world that something inside me felt broken.

The car windows were steaming up. I didn't want to think about what was going on inside, I mean we've all seen *Titanic*— or maybe you haven't, so imagine a hand slapping against some glass dripping with breath and sweat and passion. Taking care not to be seen, I climbed off the wall, my back stiff and my legs sore. Everything hurt and the world was cold and even the stars seemed spiteful, sharp bits of white poking out of all the black. As I wandered back to the stalls, my foot rolled on a stone and I went over on my ankle. The noise I made surprised me because it wasn't even painful.

"Zoe?" A figure was moving toward me, away from the fire, a black silhouette against orange. I squinted. Max came into view, a can of beer in his hand. He'd tried to catch my eye a few times since the day of the photo, but I'd ignored him. No chance of that now, though. He was standing directly in front of me. "You okay?"

"Yeah. You?"

"Cold."

Silence.

I flexed my foot even though there was no pain then racked my brain for something to say.

"It's always colder when there are no clouds. Less insulation. Reminds me of sheep."

Max took a sip from the can. "What?"

"Sheep. You know. When there are clouds, it's like the world's got fur. It's warmer and all that. But when the night's clear, it's like the planet's been shaved. . . ." I caught sight of Max's confused expression and shook my head. "It's stupid."

He took another swig. "No, it's not."

Silence again. A firework burst into stars above our heads. We both stared at them for too long, and then at each other, and then at the ground. Max cleared his throat.

"I am sorry, you know," he said, kicking a stone between his feet. The sincerity in his voice surprised me. "It was totally out of order."

"Yeah, it was."

He booted the stone away and crossed his arms. "I deleted the picture. Wasn't easy, though."

"Forget the buttons?"

That made him smile. Crooked. Off-kilter. "No, actually. It wasn't easy because you looked good."

"Really?" I replied, doing my best to sound indifferent. "That's not what you said before."

"The Mighty Max Morgan lied before." I grinned reluctantly as his eyes flicked to my chest. "Honestly, you looked . . ."

"Drunk," I finished, my heart beating faster. "Really drunk. I was almost sick on your carpet."

"I *was* sick on my carpet," Max said. "When you left, I threw up near the rug. Unless it was yours."

"No chance!" I exclaimed.

Max waggled his finger in my face. "I think you're lying."

"Think what you like," I replied, and it was remarkable. I mean, who knew that vomit could be flirtatious?

The stars seemed kinder. Softer. More golden than white and the black sky sort of blue. Max took one last drink then threw it into a trash can. He leaned against it, his legs outstretched and crossed at the ankles. The laces of his sneakers trailed in the mud.

"So, are you still in a mood with me?" he asked after a pause. A rocket shot into the sky. We both glanced at the silver sparks. And then at each other. And this time we didn't look away.

"Of course," I said. "You were an idiot."

"An idiot who you kissed first."

"An idiot who took advantage of me when I was drunk," I replied, but I took a step forward.

Max put his hand on his heart. "It won't happen again. Honest. Next time you're wearing nothing but your bra, I swear I won't—"

"Next time?!" I exclaimed, moving even closer. "How do you know there'll be a next time?"

"Just a feeling," Max whispered, and he pulled me between his legs and kissed me hard.

Not hard enough. I put my hand on the back of his head and forced our mouths closer, and I thought for some unknown reason of glass dripping with breath and sweat and passion. Max pushed his hands inside my top, over my hips, and onto my back, his fingers cold against my spine. I flicked my tongue against his, pushing myself closer, his leg disappearing between both of mine. The friction there felt good, and my back arched in a way it never had before, sort of like a cat's. A mouth moved from my lips to my cheek to my neck, and fingers crept up my ribs to the bottom of my bra. Inside my bra. Strong hands squeezed, and he grinned as I gasped. My body was tingling and my blood was throbbing, but Mum was on her way so I forced myself to twist free.

"Not here." It came out in a pant. Max dragged me toward an empty children's play area. I dug my heels into the grass. "Not tonight. My mum's probably waiting in the parking lot."

"Tomorrow, then?" he asked. I hesitated because I knew I'd never be allowed. "Or the next day?" He actually sounded nervous. Max Morgan. Nervous because of me. Lauren would never believe it.

I lifted one shoulder, unable to resist. "Yeah, why not?" He kissed me again, softer this time, but I pulled away. "I'm going to be late." Max groaned but took my hand. An image of Mum behind the steering wheel flashed into my mind. "Don't worry about walking me to the parking lot or anything. Honestly."

"It's okay. I'm leaving anyway."

I dropped his hand. "You go first, then. My mum's a bit—"

"Moody? Must run in the family." Max smirked as I elbowed him in the ribs. We walked part of the way then stopped behind a tree. Max glanced into the parking lot. "If you don't hear from me tomorrow, call an ambulance. My brother's giving me a lift home. Only passed his test a couple of weeks ago. First time, obviously. Don't think he's ever failed anything in his life. Doesn't mean he's a good driver, though. Seriously, tell your mum to be careful."

I smiled as he ran off, jogging past Mum's Mini, ignoring a Jeep, and hurrying straight to the car parked underneath the streetlight.

An old blue car with steamy windows.

I leaned closer, my heart stopping as Max pulled open the back door and climbed into the seat behind Aaron.

Now, Mr. Harris, there is this word called *flabbergasted*, and it's the only way to describe how I felt as I stood there in the darkness. My flabber was still pretty much gasted when I got home and made a cup of tea far too strong because I kept dunking the bag and dunking the bag, trying to get my head around it all. Brothers. *Brothers.* Maybe I should have seen it coming. There were slight similarities between them, and Aaron had been at Max's party even though he must have been a couple of years older than the rest of us if he could drive. . . . Still. It wasn't a lot to go on.

Steam rose from my cup as I sat on the living room carpet and sipped tea, wondering if the brothers were close and if they were chatting in the kitchen right at that moment, making a sandwich or something. I tried to work out if they'd have the same filling or different ones, Max choosing ham and Aaron opting for cheese and the girl with long red hair going for tuna that would made her breath stink of fish. I'd have given a lot to be a fly on the wall to find out the answer.

Funnily enough, there's an actual fly on the actual wall right now. Sort of. A little black one is caught in the web on the shed windowsill, stuck in the silk and staring at the garden, probably wondering what on earth happened to its freedom. By the time the sun rises, I bet the spider will have eaten it. Judging by the sky, dawn's not far off, so I probably should get back inside before Mum wakes up. Now the clocks have gone back, it's getting light an hour earlier, and Stuart that must be some consolation. Even if you have dinner in the dark, you get breakfast in the sunshine, and I hope it feels warm on your skin.

From,
Zoe x
1 Fiction Road
Bath, UK

S. Harris #993765

Polunsky Unit (Death Row)

Livingston, Texas 77351

USA
November 14

Hi Stuart,

Don't judge me, because it really wasn't my fault and I would never have agreed to go if Mum hadn't started getting suspicious. When I got back from school, she was on the phone. Don't ask me how I knew she was talking to Sandra, but I just did, and she was making these noises, "Ahah, mmm, yeah," and then she hung up and told me we were going to her house for coffee.

Of course I protested.

"I don't even like coffee."

"What's the big deal?" Mum asked, her eyes narrowing as if she were trying to send a search beam into my brain. "It might help you to see her. And I know she'd appreciate it. You like her, don't you?"

"Yeah. It's . . . I've . . . I've got a sore throat, that's all."

Mum pushed a couple of painkillers into my mouth then ushered me out of the house. Quarter of an hour later, I was sitting in Sandra's tiny sunroom for the first time since the funeral.

"Are you getting out much?" Mum asked.

"A little," Sandra replied. "Here and there." Dad wasn't kidding about her weight. Gaunt face. Jutting collarbone. Thin arms. Her hair was different, too. It used to be black with mahogany highlights, cut into layers, but the color was fading and the style had grown out. "I'm trying to keep busy."

"Good idea," Mum said. "It's the only way. Fill your time."

"I never realized there was so much of it," Sandra muttered. "Hours. I feel every minute."

The sun appeared, shining on the fountain in the garden. I saw an image of Max's finger prodding the wings of a dead moth. I blinked hard to get rid of it, but it came back stronger, and then Aaron was looking up at the owl and then Max's hand was on my thigh and then Aaron was studying my skin and lips and curves and my pulse was racing and my stomach was churning and I was just about to retch when Sandra asked, "And how are you, Zoe?" I didn't trust myself to speak.

"She's been awful," Mum said. "Her work's suffering, too."

"Well, they were close, weren't they?" Sandra said, and Stuart it was one of those rhetorical questions that didn't need an answer. "To have it all cut short like that."

82

I stood up abruptly.

"Everything okay, Zo?" Mum asked. My hands were tingling and the room was too small and my school tie was too tight. I pulled and pulled, but the knot was too stiff. "We'd better go," Mum said quickly. "She's not very well. And I've left my other two girls with a neighbor. Thanks for the brew."

Sandra climbed to her feet, her face full of concern. It hurt to look at her, so I focused on the sky as Sandra pulled my head toward her shoulder.

"I know how you feel," she said, squeezing me hard. "I really do. You're welcome here anytime." She pushed me back gently and put her hand against my cheek. "We can help each other." My fists clenched. My teeth, too. And just when I thought I couldn't stand her kindness a second longer, the hand was gone and Sandra was walking to the front door in a pair of old slippers coming apart at the seams. She paused by a picture hanging on the wall. "Have you seen this?"

A silver frame.

Me in a blue dress, my face more flushed than usual.

And Max and Aaron grinning on either side of me at the Spring Fair.

Lights from the bumper cars shone in the background. Smoke from hot dog vans hung in the air. A date in the corner said May 1.

"Is that . . . ?" Mum began.

"The last photo ever taken of him, yes." My cheeks drained of color. I actually felt it, pink trickling down my neck like face paint being washed away by cold water. "It's my favorite,"

Sandra said. "He looks so happy. You all do." With her thumb, she rubbed our three faces, and Stuart that's when I ran outside and threw up by the tree.

From,

Zoe x

1 Fiction Road

Bath, UK

S. Harris #993765

Polunsky Unit (Death Row)

Livingston, Texas 77351

USA

November 29

Hi Stuart,

Hail's banging on the shed roof, and if you never have this type
of weather in Texas then imagine heaven emptying out its
freezer. The spider must be wondering what on earth's going
on. She's standing in the middle of her empty web on jet-
black legs, and I've got the strangest feeling she's staring at me.
Probably because of my outfit. Purple woolly hat and scarf over
my dressing gown, Mum's hiking boots on my feet. I found it all
in here so Dot must have been pretending to be an explorer or
something, because she uses this shed for her playhouse. I've put
Dad's coat over my legs, sort of like a quilt, and it feels safe
under here, protection against the rain and the wind and the

disappearing hand and also Sandra's screaming, which came into my dream for the first time tonight.

I'd do anything to forget. Anything. Eat the spider or stand naked on top of the shed or do math homework every day for the rest of my life. Whatever it took to wipe my brain clean like you can with computers, pressing a button to delete the images and the words and the lies, which are just about to start in the next bit of my story, as you will see.

The day after the bonfire, my hair still smelled of smoke and my stomach was fluttery as I waited for Max to get in touch. Every single time my phone beeped, my heart went from zero to sixty in a split second like the Ferrari I'd bought for Dad. Funnily enough, we were talking about cars as we ate lunch at the kitchen table, which FYI was organic sausages and mashed potatoes.

"A new season of *Top Gear* starts tonight," I told Dad, referring to this car program he loves on TV. "Nine o'clock."

"Great," Dad said, but he didn't sound that enthusiastic. "Shall I do it now?" he asked Mum.

She sipped a glass of water and said, "If you must."

Dad put down his fork and adjusted his plate so it was in the exact middle of the mat. "We have something to tell you," he signed with difficulty. Dot was squeezing loads of ketchup onto her plate. I tapped her knee and pointed at Dad. She looked up guiltily but then saw she wasn't in trouble and pressed the bottle harder. Red spurted all over the table.

"Idiot," Soph muttered.

"We have something to tell you," Dad signed again, ignoring the mess. "Something important."

"We don't want you to worry," Mum added, but the deep line in the middle of her eyebrows undermined her words.

"Are you getting divorced?" Soph asked, holding a bit of sausage in midair. "Because you've been arguing so much?"

Mum and Dad exchanged a guilty glance.

"We haven't been arguing *that* much," Mum said.

"What's going on?" Dot signed because she sensed the tension but couldn't follow the conversation. Her fingers were red from cleaning up the ketchup.

"Mum and Dad are getting divorced," Soph signed for once. Dot's hands flew to her mouth, her knife and fork clattering onto the table.

"Sophie!" Dad snapped. "We didn't say that."

"Why are you getting divorced?" Dot signed urgently, her face covered in ketchup now. "Did Dad sex another lady?"

"What? No!" Mum replied.

"We're not getting divorced," Dad said. "I lost my job, that's all."

My jaw fell open. Money troubles I knew about, but this was news to me. Dot pulled on my sleeve. Red marks on that, too.

"Dad lost his job," I signed, struggling to believe it. Dot sighed with relief and picked up her cutlery.

"Did you get sacked?" Soph asked. "What for? Did you lose loads of money for the law firm?"

"Did you sex your boss?" Dot signed.

87

Dad exhaled slowly. "I wasn't sacked. My firm merged with another so I was made redundant."

"When are you going to get another job?" Dot asked, signing quickly. "Tomorrow? Or the next day? Or the day after that?"

"I don't know," he admitted as Dot stirred ketchup into her mashed potatoes then arranged them in blobs around the top of her plate.

"Stop playing with your food!" Mum signed.

"They're clouds," Dot replied.

"Clouds aren't red," Soph signed.

"They are at sunrise," Dot signed back defiantly. "And it's sunrise on my plate, and the sausage thinks it's lovely." She carved a smile onto the sausage with her knife.

"You're making a mess," Mum signed.

"A beautiful mess." Dot beamed. She turned around her plate to show Mum. The sausage was lying flat on its back, grinning at the ketchup clouds.

"Very nice," Mum said. "Now eat your lunch properly. There's a good girl."

Dad got up to serve the extra sausages.

"Something'll come up. There are plenty of law firms around here, and I've already started making calls. Money might be a bit tight for a while, but we'll manage."

"And if not, we could always remortgage the house," I suggested. Mum was taken aback. "Free up some funds," I went on, nodding wisely.

"Yes," Dad said, sounding impressed. "Exactly. Or your

mum could find a job." He said it without thinking, dropping a sausage onto her plate. Mum's green eyes widened so you could see all the white.

"No chance!"

"But—"

"No chance," Mum said again. "My job's at home. Here. With the girls. You lost your job. You find another."

Dad stared at Mum. Mum glared at Dad. Me and Soph looked at each other. Only Dot carried on eating, leaving the sausage with the smile to the very end of her lunch. She picked it up with her fingers and held it in front of her face. She waved solemnly as if to say good-bye then bit off its head.

Max didn't call that afternoon, and he didn't call when I was in the bath that evening. Later, I sprawled on my bedroom floor in my pajamas, trying and failing to do my French homework, poking my phone to check it was alive. I yelped as it beeped.

A message!

I rolled onto my back on top of all the French verbs I was supposed to be learning for a test. To live. To love. To laugh. To die.

My house tomorrow after school?

It was unbelievable. Actually unbelievable. I blinked twice then reread the message. Yes. There it was—an invitation to Max Morgan's house. Just for me. I wanted to thrust the phone out the window and beam his words up to the sky. Instead,

I gazed at the lamp shade, trying to think of the perfect reply. I mean, don't get me wrong, it was a no, Stuart. It had to be. Mum would never let me go to a boy's house, never in a million years. But how to word the response? Call me shallow, but I didn't want Max to lose interest, even if I did prefer his brother.

I started to type. Deleted it. Started again. Got rid of that, too. I tore out a blank page of my French notebook, and after ten minutes of scribbling, I had a reply I was happy with, plus seventeen autographs and most probably a picture of a rabbit with huge front teeth a.k.a. the only thing I can draw.

The message said I was busy but that I'd like to see him another time, and just as my thumb hovered over the SEND button, the grandfather clock struck nine.

"Dad! Dad? *Top Gear*'s about to start." There was no response. "Dad?" I said again, dropping my phone on the carpet and wandering into the hall. Light was creeping underneath the study door so I turned the handle. "*Top Gear*'s on in . . ." Dad was staring at the screen saver on the computer, his expression vacant. On the desk was a ring binder, open to a page full of his handwriting. *Holdsworth and Son. Mansons. Leighton West.* There were twenty other law firms on the list, and next to half of them, a cross.

"*Top Gear*'s about to start," I said, shaking his arm.

Dad yawned and stretched. "Record it, Zo. I'll watch it another time. I'm in the middle of something."

I thought he meant work, but when he wiggled the mouse, a picture of a couple appeared on the screen. In a crowded, smoky room, a girl had leaped into a man's arms, one leg on either side of his waist, her feet stretching toward the ceiling. Her head was thrown back, brown hair just like mine brushing the man's shiny shoes. The man was laughing, with his eyes crinkled and his mouth wide open, bending her toward the floor with powerful arms.

"Grandpa," Dad said. "And Gran. Don't they look—"

"Yeah," I muttered. "They do," because I just knew that Dad was going to say *young*.

It wasn't their faces, Stuart, and the fact that they had no wrinkles. It's hard to describe, but it was sort of their mood. Their energy. You could see it in the sweat beads on Grandpa's forehead. In the arc of Gran's back. It wasn't just dancing. It was living. Really living, like imagine the width of a moment rather than the length, and two people determined to fill every last millimeter of it.

"Makes you think, doesn't it?" Dad said.

"Definitely," I replied, and then, "Makes you think what?"

"That life's short. And there's a lot more to it than worrying."

"And school," I added, perching on the edge of the desk.

Dad chuckled. "Ah, nice try! Careful of the pictures." He tugged me off a pile of black-and-white photos. "I'm scanning them. Don't want them to fade."

I felt as if he meant *not like Grandpa* so I asked, "How is he now?"

Dad rubbed the bridge of his nose. "Not good, to be honest. His memory's shot to pieces. Last week, he couldn't even remember that he danced. I brought a few photos, but he threw them to one side and asked for his Bible and a bowl of strawberry jelly."

"He doesn't know this was him?" I asked as the young man on the screen laughed and laughed and laughed. "What about Gran? Does he remember her?"

"As an old lady, yes. But the stuff from the past has gone."

Dad sounded so fed up. I slipped out the door and returned with something hidden behind my back.

"*Ta-da.* Have this until you can afford the real thing." I waited for Dad to say thanks, but his face fell in on itself. He glanced from the Ferrari to the list of law firms on the desk. All those crosses. "I didn't mean . . . Not because you've been made redundant. That's not what I—"

"It's brilliant," Dad interrupted, taking the car and pushing it along the desk, making an engine noise in his throat, but it was halfhearted and we both knew it. "Thanks, pet," he said as the car did one of those U-turns by the ring binder and parked by the mouse.

Dad went back to the pictures, his chin resting on his hand. He clicked a button, and the dancing was replaced by a picnic in

92

the rain, a young couple on a thick rug with no sun in sight apart from the beams shining out of their smiling faces. Grandpa's hand clutched Gran's shoulder, and they were leaning against each other, their heads touching.

"Why does Mum hate him so much?" I asked. "He looks all right to me."

"She doesn't *hate* him."

"But what happened? I don't get it. Why aren't we allowed to see him?"

"Well, there was an——"

"Argument. Yeah, I know. The day of the McDonald's. But what was it about?"

Dad cleared his throat. "Don't bother yourself with all that, pet."

"But I want to know."

Dad seemed as if he might cave, but then muttered, "Some things are better left in the past."

"Some things like what?" I asked, aware I was pushing my luck.

"Now's not the time, Zoe."

"But why all the secrets? What's the big deal?"

"Look, there's no point in bringing it all up again," he snapped. "Your mum wouldn't like it."

"*Why*, though?" I said, feeling annoyed. "What did he do that was so awful?"

"Leave it!" Dad exploded. "Honestly, Zoe. Know when to back off!"

Hurt, I stormed out of the study and scooped up my phone

from the bedroom carpet. This time as I read my reply saying that I couldn't go to Max's house, my thumb didn't hover over the SEND button. It pressed DELETE. If Mum and Dad could have secrets, then so could I. Angrily, I typed three letters.

Yes.

From,
Zoe x
1 Fiction Road
Bath, UK

S. Harris #993765

Polunsky Unit (Death Row)

Livingston, Texas 77351

USA

December 3

Hi Stuart,

It's nearly Christmas. Sort of. In England, all the shops start play-ing "Jingle Bells" in November, and the Christmas lights are turned on in towns and cities on December 1. I triple-checked Google and couldn't find any information about Christmas on Death Row, but I bet the guards refuse to let you hang a stocking in your cell. Even if there is a tree in the prison, it probably doesn't feel all that festive eating gruel behind bars, and in actual fact I bet this time of year just makes everything more miserable.

That's what Sandra told me yesterday. She rang again. My heart fell when I saw her name, and honest truth I wasn't going to answer, but then I thought she might call the home phone and talk to Mum and invite us over. I picked up on pretty much the last ring as I wandered back from school underneath the flashing angels. That makes it sound as if God's messengers were showing their knickers, which would have been a whole lot more interesting than the feeble lights flickering above the main road by the church.

Sandra said she was having a bad day. Probably I was supposed to offer to visit so we could reminisce about her dead son, but Stuart I just said I had to bake something for a cake competition. It was the only thing I could think of because I was holding a Victoria sponge after my Food Technology lesson.

"A *cake* competition?" she repeated.

I suddenly panicked that my behavior sounded suspicious.

"It will be plain," I said quickly. "No icing. And probably very dry."

"Good luck with it," she replied, sounding uncertain. "And come and see me again before Christmas, won't you? This time of year makes everything so much harder to bear. It's the thought of him, really. Under the ground, when everyone else is . . . Anyway, I'd love to see you."

"Yeah, me too," I mumbled even though I had no intention of going to visit, not today or tomorrow or any day for the rest of my life even if it went on forever and ever amen.

It might sound harsh, but I don't even know her that well. If you added up all the minutes, I reckon we only spent two hours together before she was holding on to my arm at the funeral, crying silently by the coffin, her fingernails digging into my skin. The first time we came into contact was so brief it hardly counts, and Stuart I will tell you all about it right now so imagine me at school, funnily enough in the cooking classroom, struggling to make a loaf of whole wheat bread.

I lifted my eyes from the weighing scales to see the brown hair at the base of Max's neck in the classroom next to mine. My stomach flipped over and landed with a thud that shook my brain. All sensible thought sprinkled right out of it like salt, which FYI I'd forgotten to add to my bread mixture. The loaf was a disaster, flat and burned, and there was nothing for it but to chuck it away. The trash can just so happened to be by the door to the graphics classroom, and Max must have sensed my presence. When I scraped the bread off the tray with a knife, he glanced up from his design. I waved my hand, but unfortunately it was the one holding the knife, plus I was too tense to smile. From Max's point of view, I must have appeared stony-faced in the window, brandishing a sharp weapon, before vanishing a second later.

Lauren was finding it hard to believe.

"Max's house. *Max's house,*" she kept saying, and I loved the admiration in her voice. "You're actually going to *his house* tonight?"

"Thought I might as well," I said airily.

"And your mum agreed to it?" she asked, flour all over her apron.

"Not exactly." I told her how I'd lied to my parents about going to the library to do some research on rivers for a Geography project. "They're keeping secrets from me so I don't feel bad about keeping stuff from them."

"It's a slippery slope," Lauren sang, and Stuart she was so right, but I just shrugged with that word called *ignorance*, saying, "One little lie won't hurt anyone."

When the bell rang, I shoved my books into my bag and dashed to the bike shed where we'd arranged to meet, feeling sick with nerves. Max's house. *Aaron's house.* Honest truth, I almost chickened out, like imagine one of those raw birds from the supermarket in a school uniform with a look of terror on its face. But then Max turned up looking sort of perfect and before I knew it I was following him out of the school gate, hoping all the other girls could see.

But not hear. The conversation was stilted now that Max was sober. Our confidence from the bonfire had vanished like *poof* into thin air, and we were just two teenagers in school uniforms traipsing through the drizzle, no fireworks to speak of.

"What did you do yesterday?" I said as we stopped by a crosswalk and waited for the little green man.

"Played soccer."

"What was the score?"

"Three–two to us."

"Three–two to you," I repeated as the green man appeared.

"Why are you waving?" Max asked, and sure enough my hand was moving from side to side in the air. It was a habit, a thing I did to make Dot smile, saying hello to the green man like he was an actual person with an actual job and not just a light on a machine.

"Just swatting a mosquito."

"It's winter."

"A robin, then," I joked, but Max didn't get it.

When we reached his house and walked up the garden path, I made sure my feet didn't touch the alligators. Max unlocked the door, and there was absolutely no need for me to put my fingers on the handle, but in Biology we'd just learned about DNA and how it brushes off your body without you even realizing it. I squeezed the cold metal, wondering how many times Aaron had done the same.

"You coming in, then?" Max said, taking off his jacket and hanging it on a peg by the front door. I stepped into the hall as the multicolored swirls of Aaron tingled on my skin.

"So, er, do you want a drink or something? Orange juice?" he asked.

I nodded, straining my ears to see if I could hear anyone else in the house, but it was silent apart from a radiator groaning in the kitchen. We were alone. And the road outside the house was empty.

"Where's your mum?" I asked, though it wasn't her car I was thinking about.

"Work," Max said, pouring two juices in the kitchen. It was small with a table in one corner and two plants dying on the windowsill.

"And your dad?"

"Doesn't live with us."

"Oh yeah. You said. Sorry," I added, because Max's face had clouded over.

"Whatever. Doesn't bother me." He handed me a glass. "He left a couple of years ago so I'm pretty used to it." I downed my juice in one go. Max did the same. Our glasses clinked as we dropped them in the sink, and a dog barked outside. "Mozart. Stupid name for a dog."

"They should've called it Bach," I said, grinning. Max didn't reply so I just asked where the toilet was, despite the fact I didn't need to go and I already knew the answer from the party.

"I'll show you," he said, leading me to the upstairs bathroom. He made an awkward noise, staring at something by the silver flush. I followed his gaze to see a tube of cardboard hanging on the wall where a toilet roll should have been. "Er . . . I'll get you some more."

"No need," I replied. Max raised his eyebrows. I had no intention of doing anything on the toilet, but he didn't know that.

"You sure?"

"Yes. I mean no. I need a roll," I said. Max's eyebrows lifted even further. "Not a whole roll," I added. "Just one piece."

In case Max was listening, I made the pretense of going to the bathroom, flushing the toilet and turning on the tap. The bar of soap had shrunk to the size of a fifty-pence coin, and I imagined Aaron washing his hands so I bent down to smell it. My lungs filled with the scent of him. I picked up the soap and dropped it into my coat pocket. Probably I'm sounding crazy right now, but people do all sorts of weird things, e.g., on this TV program that put hidden cameras in public places, a middle-aged woman in the bathroom of a posh restaurant fox-trotted toward the hand dryer, swooning underneath the heat, saying, "Oh, Johnny," like she was in that film *Dirty Dancing*. And once, when Mum took me to London to see a musical just before Dot was born, she dragged me to this place where the Beatles crossed the road, which sounds like a joke but actually happened in real life, on the front of an album cover, to be precise.

There were loads of tourists clicking their cameras and risking death by posing on the crossing, trying to dodge the red buses. The tourists were giddy, but Mum was the giddiest one of all, if you can believe that, posing for a photo with her arm wrapped around a man from Wokingham dressed like John Lennon. I reckon that woman in the restaurant would have picked up Patrick Swayze's soap, and that man from Wokingham would have picked up John Lennon's soap so Stuart I don't think I was all that weird for picking up Aaron's soap. I bet you did some peculiar things when you fell in love with Alice after your first date at the diner. Perhaps you took a ketchup packet off the table and even when you ran out of tomato sauce at home you could never bring yourself to open it, and maybe it's still in your cupboard now between the mustard and the Worcestershire sauce.

Anyway, time's ticking so I'd better get my skates on, like imagine my fingers wrapped up warm for winter and this letter all frozen as my hand slides across it. Suffice to say things were getting heavy in Max's room. His fingers were creeping toward the zip of my school skirt when I heard a car park outside, and *BAM*, all of a sudden I came to my senses.

"Where are you going?" Max moaned because I'd jumped off the bed, straightening my clothes.

I pretended to look at my phone then put it on his desk. "Places to be." I pulled on my shoes and ran my fingers through my hair as the front door opened and closed.

"You don't have to rush off," Max said. "I'm allowed to have girls around."

"I really should go," I replied, imagining Aaron's face when he saw me with his brother. A bag was dropped at the foot of the stairs and a TV was turned on.

"Come on, Zoe. Stay a bit." He patted the bed by his side, then faked a shiver. "I'm getting cold without you."

"Do up your shirt, then," I snapped, which he did in a sulk, taking an age over it as I hovered in the middle of the room, desperate to leave but trying to hide it.

"You're no fun," he muttered, standing up at last.

We made our way downstairs.

"That you, Max?" someone called over the sound of the TV. Someone female. I breathed a sigh of relief.

"No, Mum. It's a burglar nicking all your stuff," he deadpanned.

"Oh, ha-ha. Very funny. School okay?"

"Same as always," Max called back. "Math. Boring. English. Boring. Science. Boring."

"Easy with the enthusiasm there, sweetheart. Aaron back yet?"

I flinched, then rubbed my nose to disguise it.

"Nah. He's probably at Anna's."

Anna. So that was her name. I opened the door, feeling suddenly flat.

"See you later," I said as Max kissed my cheek.

"Aren't you going to introduce me to whoever is lurking in my hall?" his mum called.

"Maybe another time," Max replied, and that was that, my first contact with Sandra over and done with.

Now, if you were a nosy neighbor on Max's street, you would have been sorely disappointed because absolutely nothing happened as we said good-bye in the garden. I waved and Max waved and he closed the door quickly, and honest truth the whole thing had been a bit of a damp squib, and if you don't know what that is then picture a soggy explosive that fails to go off and you're pretty much on the right lines.

By the time I left the house, the moon was shining in the indigo sky. I would love to say it was one of those full ones to make it seem significant, but it wasn't particularly twinkling or romantic so I had no clue that something amazing was about to happen. That something amazing turned out to be an old blue car waiting at a traffic light by the church. A pigeon flew out of nowhere so I ducked as it almost hit my head, and when I straightened up, someone beeped a horn. My eyes adjusted to the dazzle of the headlights, and I realized with a great rush of adrenaline that it was Aaron.

"Bird Girl!" he called from the car. "Hanging out with pigeons!"

"Getting attacked by them," I corrected him.

"Well, I'd better give you a lift, then!"

I don't think I even gave a reply, just ran into the road as the traffic light turned green and a man in a van yelled angrily through his open window. Holding up my hand to apologize, I dived into DORIS headfirst. Aaron sped off before I'd closed the door. Caught up in my seat belt, my face somewhere near the hand brake as we screeched forward, my nose banged against Aaron's thigh. We started to laugh.

"Pull in somewhere," I said, my sides aching, my foot stuck under my thigh. "I've got pins and needles!"

Aaron stopped by the Chinese takeout. "Hi," he said when I was sitting normally.

"Hi," I replied, and a dry squib exploded in the darkness between us. Aaron was wearing faded jeans and a baggy blue sweater, and his blond hair wasn't doing anything special but looked pretty much perfect sitting there on top of his head.

"So, where're we going?" Aaron asked.

Someplace far away. That's what I wanted to say, and Timbuktu was the first thing that popped into my head, but of course I just asked for a lift to Fiction Road, because I knew Mum would be waiting. Aaron checked over his shoulder and pulled off as a woman in the Chinese takeout flipped a sign on the door. OPEN. The lights came on and a dragon in the window shone green, making me think of adventures in faraway lands, and I wished harder than I'd wished for most things in my life that the car was magic and could take us all the way to Timbuktu, because at the time I thought it was a mythical place sort of like Narnia rather than an actual town in Africa, blighted by poverty and famine.

"Fiction Road it is," Aaron said, except of course he used my real address, and I loved how he knew where my house was and didn't have to ask for directions.

Once Dad read this book about the adaptability of humans and how we are remarkable creatures because we can get used to anything, and, Stuart, that is so true if you consider how people fall asleep on planes, not even thinking about how miraculous it is to be high up in the sky, flying above the clouds to South America or somewhere, going to the loo thousands of miles above the earth, peeing all over the ocean. And that's what it was like driving along with Aaron. At first it was *Whoooaaaaa* but after a few minutes I got used to it and I had the strangest sense that on that seat was where I belonged. We drove effortlessly down the long road, and the traffic lights turned green at the right moment as if the dragon from the restaurant was breathing emerald fire to illuminate our way home.

Aaron glanced at my uniform.

"Bath High?" he said. "I used to go there. My brother still does."

"Really?" I said, my face interested but my insides turning cold. Liver. Spleen. Heart. Everything froze.

"Max Morgan. You know him?" Aaron turned right. Sped down a clear road. Slowed down and turned left.

"Max..." I started, but an ambulance roared up behind us, sirens blaring. Aaron swerved out of the way, his foot slamming the brake as something hard hit the glass by my head. A tiny red figure swung from the rearview mirror, tapping against the window. I rested it on the palm of my hand as the ambulance hurtled down the road and disappeared around a bend.

"That was close!" Aaron breathed.

"Is this—"

"The Miss Scarlet player piece from Clue," Aaron confirmed. "And Clue dice. Everyone at college had those lame fluffy things so I thought I'd hang actual dice from my mirror instead. Besides, Clue rocks."

"You like Clue?"

"Do you like Clue?"

"I love it," we replied at the exact same moment, and then we grinned.

"So much better than Monopoly. All that going around in a circle..." Aaron said.

"Passing Go..."

"Stealing money from the bank to buy houses..." Aaron finished. "Everyone steals a little bit," he protested as I looked horrified.

"I don't!"

"'Course you do."

"Honestly I don't!"

"You've never stolen Monopoly money?" Aaron asked. "You haven't lived. I'll show you how to do it sometime."

"Sure." I shrugged, but inside my heart was thawing, dripping all over my bones.

The sign for Fiction Road came into view, black letters on a white post that had a fat brown cat sitting on top of it, maybe the same one I can hear outside the shed right now, meowing in the darkness. We were getting closer and the cat's eyes were getting brighter, but I didn't want to go home, not yet, not ever.

"Stop here a second," I said.

Aaron pretended to tip a chauffeur's hat as he pulled up next to the cat. "Let's say hello!"

"What . . . No . . . *Wait!*" I called, but Aaron had already disappeared, leaving the car door wide open.

"Hello, Mr. Cat," he said, stroking the speck of white between the cat's pointy ears.

"Lloyd," I corrected him. "He lives next door. Along with Webber."

"Lloyd Webber," Aaron muttered as the cat jumped off the sign and rubbed his head against my leg with a pebbly sort of purr. "We've got a dog next door to us called Mozart."

I nodded as if this was brand-new information. "They should've called it Bach," I joked, but my heart wasn't really in it. Aaron laughed, and the sound made me happy and sad, like Stuart imagine those faces from the theater hanging from my ribs in the middle of my stomach.

"Beautiful animals," Aaron muttered as the cat shot off into the bushes. "Don't you think?"

I climbed onto the wall, shivering slightly. "I don't know. I prefer dogs."

Aaron jumped up next to me. "Cats are definitely better. More free. Like Lloyd, just running off to explore."

"But they're always on their own. Dogs are more sociable. Wagging their tails. Running about."

"Cats can climb trees," Aaron argued.

"But dogs can swim. And cats kill birds, which I just couldn't do."

"You and your birds," Aaron said, lifting one foot onto the wall and resting his arms on his bent knee.

"I love them. Better than cats and dogs and all the other animals put together."

"What's so special about them?" Aaron asked, turning to look at me as if he was extremely interested in the answer.

I thought for a while. "Well, they can fly."

Aaron gasped. "Really?"

I hit him on the arm. "Don't be an idiot! I won't tell you if—"

"No, go on," he said, his eyes twinkling.

"Well, they can fly"—I glanced at him suspiciously, but he

remained silent—"which is unbelievable; I mean, imagine being able to take off and go wherever you wanted. Like swallows. It's crazy how far they go."

"They're the ones that migrate?" Aaron asked.

I sat on my hands and nodded. "They fly away for winter, these tiny little things zooming above the ocean, totally fearless. Twenty thousand miles they travel, or something, and then they fly all the way back again when the world's a bit warmer. I don't know. It's sort of cool," I finished feebly.

Aaron reached out and squeezed my thigh. "Really cool," he said. Electricity shot up my leg and buzzzzzed in my body long after he'd let go. "So, what're you up to this weekend?" he asked, working hard to sound casual.

I worked even harder in my reply. "Stacking shelves in the library where I work. How about you?"

"Writing an essay. Really dull."

"I've got loads of homework, too. My mum's putting the pressure on, going on about grades and how I need to do well if I want to go into law."

"Do you want to go into law?" Aaron asked, folding his arms.

I wrinkled my nose. "Not really. But Mum and Dad are both lawyers so . . ."

"So what?"

"Well, it's a good job, isn't it?"

"Depends on your definition of *good*," Aaron said. "Personally, I can't imagine anything worse. Sitting in an office all day. Paperwork. Staring at a computer screen."

Scared he was starting to think I was boring, I said,

"Actually, my dream job is to write children's books." I'd never expressed it so boldly before and immediately felt daft. "Not that I've got any chance of doing it. Not really."

"Hey, don't say that! You're too young to be cynical."

"Not cynical. Realistic. Writing doesn't pay," I said, echoing Mum.

"According to J.K. Rowling, it does."

I laughed. "Trust me, my story is not as good as Harry Potter."

"So you're writing something? Tell me about it."

"No chance!"

"Chicken." He started to quack and flap his elbows like wings.

"Aaron, that's a duck."

He cracked a smile. "I might not be a bird expert, but I know a coward when I see one."

"Fine. It's called *Bizzle the Bazzlebog. . . .*"

"Good title."

"But it's for little kids, ten-year-olds or something, so it will probably sound really—"

"Just spit it out!"

After a pause, I took a deep breath and spoke as fast as I could.

"Okay, so Bizzle is this blue furry creature who lives in a tin of baked beans but then one day a boy called Mod fancies beans on toast so he opens the tin and pours them into a bowl but Bizzle plops out and I've never said that to anyone so I don't want you to react in any way." He did as he was told. Literally. Sat

110

there completely still without breathing. I rolled my eyes. "Okay, maybe you can react a little bit."

"Phew," he exhaled. "I was beginning to suffocate." He shoved me playfully with his shoulder. "It sounds good."

"What's your plan, then?" I said to change the subject, turning to face him by straddling the wall.

"My plan? I don't have one."

"Everyone's got a plan," I said in surprise.

"Not me."

"So what, you're just going to leave college and then—"

"And then"—Aaron waved his hand through the air—"see what happens. Think about it for a while. There's no rush, is there?"

Picking some moss with my finger, I tried to picture Aaron in thirty years' time. Serious. Weary. Gray hair above his ears like Dad. It was impossible. Especially when he stood up on the wall and pulled me to my feet. I gripped his arm to keep from falling over.

"I like climbing walls," he announced suddenly.

"Er...I like climbing walls, too," I said, struggling to balance.

"I like winter and I like the dark and I like cats and I like the rain and I like walking up mountains and sitting at the top in the fog. That's all I need to know about my life right now. It's pretty simple. And I can experience it all for free."

"But you need money," I argued. "Everyone needs money."

"True. But just enough to survive. And maybe a tiny bit left over to have an adventure. That's what I'm going to do when I leave college, actually. Go off somewhere. My dad gave me some money on my seventeenth birthday to buy a car with a personalized license plate. I don't think DOR1S is exactly what he had in mind. But she was cheap, and she works well enough. And I've saved the rest to do something fun."

"This is fun," I said without thinking about it, wondering if this is how Mum and Dad had felt at the very beginning, when they used to write each other love letters.

"Yeah," Aaron said, tilting back his head in the drizzle. "It really is."

Just when I thought the night couldn't get any more perfect, an image of a parking lot forced itself into my mind. A parking lot with two people walking through it. Stopping by the streetlight. Embracing in the amber glow.

"I should go," I said suddenly, jumping off the wall, the moment ruined. "Mum said I had to be back by six."

Aaron stayed where he was, throwing out his arms and balancing on one leg. "Good thing I gave you a lift. You'd have been late. What were you doing over there, anyway?"

"Sorry?" I said, though I'd heard him just fine. I dusted down my school skirt, not meeting his eyes.

"Why were you in that part of town after school? I live around there."

"Visiting my grandpa," I murmured, flicking nonexistent dirt off the material.

"What road does he live on?"

I couldn't think of a single street so I just said, "He's buried in the graveyard by the traffic lights."

"Oh. Sorry."

"Don't be. He's at peace," and Stuart it was sort of true, because sitting in a hospital asking for strawberry jelly wasn't exactly stressful.

Aaron hopped off the wall. I opened the passenger door. His bicep tensed as he grabbed my bag. Our fingers brushed together as he handed me the strap. Ten seconds later, he was still handing me the strap, my fingers tingling with all his multicolored DNA.

"So, this is the part where you give me your number," Aaron whispered. "Without me having to ask for it." My heart leaped, but I hesitated, thinking of the girl with long red hair. "Or you can take mine? You know. Just to arrange the bank robbery."

I grinned. I couldn't help it. I didn't know my number so I shoved my hand into my bag, searching for my phone. Schoolbooks. Pens. An elastic band. I moved my fingers into the very corners. Paper clip. Chewing gum. A lid from a bottle.

"It's not there," I said, confused, and then I gasped.

"Where is it?"

"I . . . I must've left it at school."

Aaron grabbed a pen out of the glove box. He took my hand, writing his number on my palm, the nib tickling my skin as zeros and sevens and sixes and eights spread from my thumb to my little finger across my life line and my love line and all the other creases that gypsies read in caravans. Black ink shone in the moonlight, but all I could see was my phone in Max's bedroom. On his desk. With a picture of me and Lauren as the screen saver. I pulled my hand away and lifted my bag onto my shoulder. A crease formed between Aaron's eyebrows, and I wanted to jump right in and fluff it up like a pillow.

"Is everything okay?" he asked, and Stuart this was an impossible question, but for the second time that evening, I was spared the need to answer by an ambulance.

The same ambulance we'd seen just a few minutes before.

It was turning out of Fiction Road—*my* road—blue lights flashing.

Now I don't know if you've ever been in a hospital waiting room, but if you ask me, it's the worst place in the entire world. There was a battered sofa and a sticky coffee table and an overflowing trash can and an empty water dispenser and a droopy plant that looked more ill than all the patients in the ward put together. Cigarette butts were squashed into the plant's dry soil even though there were six NO SMOKING signs and one poster about lung cancer with graphic images of tumors. Next to the poster was a stack of pamphlets about bladder weakness, which could explain why the nurses hadn't refilled the water.

Voices sounded outside the room. Soph scrambled to her feet and pushed open the door, but it wasn't Mum or Dad or Dot, just a couple of doctors marching past with stethoscopes around their necks, white coats swishing. A siren sounded in the distance and a metal trolley clattered onto the pavement and somewhere close by a heart monitor went *beeeeeeeeeeep*. I prayed and prayed that it wasn't Dot's.

I'm sure you've heard of something called sixth sense, a feeling that scratches your brain to tell you someone you love is in danger, and Stuart maybe you get it in your cell, like if your

114

brother who I'm guessing you don't want to talk about has a sore throat then perhaps your tonsils sting, too. Well, as soon as I'd spotted the ambulance, I started to run. Aaron shouted after me, but I didn't even look back because I just knew that something was wrong. Sure enough, when I sprinted toward the drive, Soph was standing there, crying and muttering something about our sister.

Mum had traveled in the ambulance with Dot, telling Soph to stay behind. Well, I wasn't having any of that so I called a taxi and we leaped in.

"She fell," Soph said, tears splashing down her face. "Right from the top to the bottom."

"Of what?" I asked in a whisper.

"The stairs. She was just lying there on the carpet and she wasn't moving and..." The sentence hung in the air as we arrived at the hospital, where a nurse with a stern face took us to the waiting room.

After forever, the hinges of the door creaked and there was Mum, standing in the doorway, her top hanging out of her jeans.

"How's Dot?" I asked.

"Is she okay?" Soph whispered.

Mum collapsed onto a chair. "It's..."

"It's what?" I said, gripping Soph's arm.

Mum sighed heavily. "A broken wrist."

"A broken wrist?" Soph asked.

"*Just* a broken wrist?" I said.

We all jumped as the door opened a second time. Dad came in carrying a briefcase, pink-faced and panting in the expensive black suit he only ever used for meetings with important clients or funerals.

"I got your message! What happened? How's Dot?"

"She's broken her wrist."

"Oh, thank God," Dad said.

"Thank God?"

"Well, I thought from what you said on the message that . . . Anyway, is she okay?"

Mum stared at her lap. "It's my fault. I should have been watching her."

"You can't watch her all the time," Dad said gently. "Not all the time."

"She fell down the stairs. She must've tripped on a bit of tinsel. I don't know why she was wearing it, but she tripped and just . . . *fell*. Knocked herself out. I couldn't wake her, Simon, and she was just lying there like last time, hardly breathing and . . ."

Dad crouched down in front of her. "It's not your fault, pet. Accidents happen."

Mum took a deep, shaky breath and nodded as Dad rubbed her cheek. "How did you get on, anyway?" she asked, taking in Dad's suit. "Any luck?"

"Down to the last two, but they gave the job to the other guy."

Before Mum could reply, light from the corridor burst into the waiting room. A nurse held open the door to reveal Dot with a cast on her hand, silver tinsel sparkling around her neck. Soph was the first to reach her, falling to her knees and signing urgently, faster than I knew she could. I missed what she was saying, but Dot nodded and Soph pulled her into a rare hug. Dad picked her up and squeezed her tight and Mum said, "Careful, Simon," and then we went home, and Stuart I know that's abrupt, but there's a cat meowing at the shed door so just a sec because I'm going to let him in.

Sorry, but I better cut this short because it's impossible to write with Lloyd purring on my lap, getting in the way of the paper. The white speck between his ears is softer than ever before, and I keep touching it and putting my lips there, too. I wanted to say how Mum and Dad had a row about Dot when we got back from the hospital. And I wanted to tell you how I wrapped my palm in a plastic bag to protect Aaron's number in the shower. And I wanted to describe how I hid under my covers and held my hand to my ear, pretending to dial an imaginary phone and speak to him in the darkness. My words traveled through my veins, which hung in the sky like telephone wires. I explained about the phone in Max's room and he explained about the girlfriend, and of course we forgave each other, lying there all night whispering love through our wrists in the pale glow of the unremarkable moon.

From,

Zoe x

1 Fiction Road

Bath, UK

S. Harris #993765

Polunsky Unit (Death Row)

Livingston, Texas 77351

USA

December 20

Hey Stuart,

Yesterday I made you a card, but don't worry, there are no pictures of families eating turkey or twinkling Christmas lights or snowmen grinning with happiness made out of stones that can't erode. None of that festive cheer felt appropriate so I drew a bird instead, a red-tailed hawk flying above your cell, which according to Google is roughly the same size as my garden shed, but it doesn't have watering cans or a jacket or a box of tiles that cuts into your thighs, and it probably doesn't smell of Dad's old sneakers, either. In actual fact there's nothing much in your cell at all except a bed in one corner with a very thin mattress and a toilet at the opposite end of the room. If you ask me, that's not very hygienic, and you should think about complaining to the people in charge of health and safety, or maybe writing a protest poem for the website.

Last week I read your poem "Verdict," and according to verse two, you didn't cry when the judge said *Guilty*. You didn't shout out in anger when your brother cheered and you didn't cry out in terror when you were escorted to the prison, because your mind was floating above the whole thing, looking down on a man in handcuffs. Honest truth, I know exactly what you mean because yesterday my brain was hovering with a pigeon near an oak tree, watching a girl in a black coat write words on a white rectangle of card.

I felt not-there as we walked to the grave and I felt not-there when we laid down our wreaths and I felt not-there as Sandra put her hand on the marble headstone and traced the gold engravings with a gloved finger.

"We'll never forget you," she whispered, and Stuart I could see his brown eyes staring up at me as she read out the words on her wreath. "Always on my mind. Always in my heart. Happy Christmas, my darling son."

It was my turn to speak. I opened my lips that weren't my lips. "Happy Christmas." The words on the coffin lid started to burn, the heat of the truth rising up from the ground, making me flush.

I didn't want to be there. I would never have gone if Sandra hadn't turned up at my house earlier that day, ringing the door-bell three times.

"Is Zoe in?" I heard her say from my bedroom.

"Er, yes," Mum said, taken aback. "Yes, she is. Why don't you come in, Sandra?"

"I won't stay, thanks. I just want to talk to Zoe."

Mum started on the stairs so I threw myself on the carpet to see if there was space to hide underneath my bed. Mum poked her head around the door before I could disappear. Of course I went downstairs and of course I was polite and of course I said yes when she asked me to visit the grave, even though my brain screamed NO so loud I was surprised she couldn't hear it.

"You sure, my love?" Mum said, looking concerned, and I tried to tell her with my eyes that I didn't want to go.

"Of course she is," Sandra replied. She was even thinner, Stuart, her face a skull and her fingers bones. "She wants to see him, don't you?" I didn't dare refuse so I swallowed and nodded, finding it hard to breathe. Anger flooded my veins. Guilt, too. They curdled in my stomach, making it ache, and it's still hurting now, a dull throb in my intestines, like maybe he wrote the truth there, too. Stuart, I know it sounds crazy, but that's how it feels sometimes, like the words are clawed on my insides, red and sore and swollen. The only way to make them disappear, to soothe the pain, is to write them down here. Tell them to you. I'm tired tonight, but I'll do it anyway, starting with the day after Dot's accident.

I was balancing on the porch step, bracing myself for the weather, when Mum said she'd give me a lift to school.

"I don't want you catching a cold on top of everything else."

Her face was pinched and bags hung under her eyes as we set

off through the rain—proper English rain falling in lines, not dots, from jet-black clouds. She was driving so slowly a neighbor beeped to tell us to get out of the way. Mum jumped and muttered under her breath, all grumpy as if she'd been tossing and turning on her pillow without any sleep, not even the tiniest wink of it.

Windshield wipers sloshed and tires splattered through puddles and Lloyd was running along the pavement, fur stuck to his bones, half the size of the fat thing that had been slumped on the sign. My heart ached with how much I wanted to be back on the wall, saying, "At least dogs aren't stupid enough to go out in the rain." For the hundredth time, I wondered if Aaron had seen my phone and if he'd had a huge argument with Max, probably ending up with one of them punching the other.

Mum was sitting so far forward, her head was hanging over the steering wheel. Dot was strapped firmly into the backseat, grimacing and holding her wrist and glancing at Mum to see if she'd noticed. Mum had given her the day off from school, and Soph had tried it on, too, complaining about a stomachache, but Mum had checked her out before we'd left the house.

"You look fine to me. And your temperature's normal."

When we dropped Soph outside the gate of her primary school, she barely said good-bye, just traipsed down the drive as Dot waved cheerfully out of the car window with the arm that was supposed to be hurting.

The first time I spotted Max that day was in the lunch hall, and honest truth he took my breath away, which was a surprise, like one second I was inhaling quite normally and the next my lungs stopped working as he walked in with a soccer ball under his arm, his dark hair dripping wet. We smiled at each other in the queue as the lunch lady yelled, "Next, please!"

"A salad?" Lauren said as I picked up a bowl of leafy stuff. "You hate salad."

I stared at her pointedly. "No, I don't. I love it."

Lauren stared right back, completely oblivious to Max's presence. "In History, you told me you were so hungry you'd eat your own grandpa if he was battered and came with a side order of fries and mushy peas."

Max smiled as I looked mortified, but I swapped the salad on my tray for a plate of proper food.

For the rest of lunch, I sat with Lauren in our homeroom as the radiators blasted hot, dry heat. As we doodled in our diaries, I filled her in about Max but not Aaron, making her laugh about the toilet roll and exaggerating the awkwardness with his mum in the hall. Max felt less personal somehow, more of a story, but Aaron was too private to say out loud. The party and the bonfire and the car journey, all of it had happened under the cover of darkness so it was hard to expose, especially in a classroom with boys chucking a Frisbee underneath the fluorescent strip lights. Lauren drew a house and I drew a smiley face and she drew a heart and I drew a wonky dog and cat, wrapping their tails together in a big bow.

"Cute," Lauren yawned, tipping back her head with her mouth wide open, the Frisbee flying out of nowhere to smack her on the nose.

Lauren stumbled into the nurse's office as I waited outside, picking up a pamphlet about teenage pregnancy. *How To Tell Your Parents.* That's what I was reading when I heard a shuffling noise behind me. I spun around to see Max glance at the pamphlet, his eyes widening in alarm even though we hadn't come close to doing it.

"I got a visit from this person called Gabriel. Bright. Big wings."

Max looked puzzled, then amused. "I don't always get your jokes, but I like that you tell them."

He collapsed on the floor with his leg outstretched, mud smeared all over his school shirt, his aftershave mixing with the smell of grass and rain. Three girls in the year below scuttled past as Max pulled down his sock, giggling and whispering and holding on to each other in this helpless sort of adoration. His foot was puffy so I touched it gently, glancing at the girls. Sure enough, their eyes turned into daggers, and I liked the way the blades twinkled in my direction.

"That feels good," Max murmured, so I did it again.

"You don't have my phone, do you?" I asked. "Did I leave it at yours?"

Max shut his eyes and gritted his teeth. "Yeah. It's in my locker. Meet me there after school?" Nothing in his voice told me that his brother had found the phone, and when I looked closely at his face, there were no bruises, either.

"See you there," I said happily, and Max returned my smile.

Of course, I had absolutely no intention of kissing him again when the final bell rang, but I didn't get much choice in the

123

matter, like Stuart imagine a strong mouth attaching itself to yours and firm hands pushing your back against a wall. Now that I come to think of it, you might have experienced this already, because unfortunately I've heard the rumors about what goes on in male prisons. Even as I tried to protest, Max's lips clamped against mine and my words got lost in all our saliva, but I have to admit I didn't try very hard to find them again.

That night Mum and Dad had another argument that turned into a row that lasted all week, in the kitchen and the living room and the bathroom as Mum brushed her teeth so hard I thought she might knock them out. Dad wanted Mum to get a job, and Mum was point-blank refusing.

"But the girls don't need you as much now that they're older!" Dad said for the twentieth time on Saturday morning, waking me up.

"Look what happened to Dot!" Mum replied, spitting out noisily in the sink. "I have to be at home!"

"Who for, exactly?"

"What's that supposed to mean?"

"The girls are at school, Jane. They don't need you during the day so who are you staying here for, eh?"

The tap came on.

"I'm a mum, aren't I? It's my job to stay at home!"

"You can be a mum and work in an office. Part-time, especially. You don't have to be here every second of the day. You used to juggle both things."

"And look what happened then!" Mum shouted, and I had no idea what she meant so I sat up in bed, listening closely. "Look what happened when I went back to work, Simon!" Glass smashed against tiles as she yanked open the shower door. "I'm not risking it. Now can you please give me some space so I can get ready?"

Soph appeared at the end of my bed in pajamas, her hair sticking up in all directions.

"They don't love each other anymore."

I pulled the duvet over my head as the shower came on full blast, determined to enjoy the last bit of bed before my shift at the library.

"'Course they do," I said, though I didn't sound sure. "It's just buried."

"Buried under what?"

"Money worries and job worries and Grandpa worries . . ." I trailed off, wondering if it happened to every couple. How it happened. When. For some reason, I thought of Gran and Grandpa in the black-and-white pictures and Dad's love letters to Mum. Gold silk hair. Calm-rock-pool eyes. Starlight confidence.

"I don't ever want to grow up," Soph interrupted, which is exactly what I was thinking. She flopped onto my bed. "Not ever."

"You want to stay nine years old for the rest of your life?" I asked from underneath the covers.

"No. Definitely not. Nine's the worst."

"So you don't want to be a child, but you don't want to be an adult?" I clarified.

"Right. I want to be a . . . what's left?"

I pulled the duvet down. "Death." I started to laugh, but Soph didn't join in.

"I'd make a good corpse," she said after a pause, crossing her arms over her chest. "It would be nice to lie in a coffin for a bit."

"You'd get bored."

"Wouldn't."

"Would. And anyway, I'd miss you."

She held out her arms in the manner of a zombie. "I'd come back from the dead to visit you," she chanted in a spooky monotone. "Just you, though," she said in her normal voice. "Not Mum or Dad. And definitely not Dot."

At the beginning of my shift in the library, I tidied up the shelves in the History section, putting the books in chronological order. Similar to the bonfire, there was no buildup. One minute Aaron wasn't there, and the next he was, sitting at a desk just meters from where I was standing behind the shelf. Gripping the wood to steady myself, I blinked quickly probably ten times in total to make absolutely sure my eyes weren't imagining things. Through a gap in the Nazi section, my nose hovering above a swastika, I watched Aaron open his bag, get out a notepad, flick through the pages, and begin to write.

Fixing a pleasant sort of expression on my face, I started to walk toward his desk, changed my mind at the last moment, and zoomed back to the shelf, my stomach bursting with butterflies. Call me a coward, but I was scared to bound over all presumptuous when last time I'd snatched his number and sprinted off down a dark road. Besides, I hadn't called, and I didn't know how to explain that without mentioning his brother and the fact that we'd kissed in a deserted locker room for five minutes and I'd enjoyed every wet second of it.

Aaron bit the end of his pen then scribbled something in the margin. He looked up so I ducked, my fingers gripping the shelves and my heart clattering against my ribs. Slowly slowly, I straightened up once more to spy through the gap, every sinew in my neck straining as my breath quivered in my nostrils. Aaron was writing again, his shoulders broad in a white T-shirt that was the brightest thing in the library and most probably the world, and I was drawn to it by a gravitational pull because this shining boy was the center of my universe, or at least more interesting than stacking books on a dusty shelf.

Squeezing my lips together, I made my way toward Aaron, but he was so engrossed in his work and my nerves were so out of control that I just sped straight past without stopping. As I stepped clumsily over his bag, my thigh almost brushed his arm, and I could hear Aaron's eyes pop out of his head with a cartoon *booooiiiiiing*. I practically ran to the front desk and lifted up the Returns box for something to do, my hands trembling against the cardboard.

I tipped it too roughly. Books clattered onto the desk. My boss, Mrs. Simpson, tutted behind the computer. *Wuthering Heights. Bleak House. The Girl Who Kicked the Hornet's Nest.* A book about the Berlin Wall and one about toads.

"Bird Girl," someone whispered, and I turned to see Aaron a few centimeters from my face. He grinned as I blushed.

"Those books won't return themselves to the shelf," Mrs. Simpson said, looking down her long nose. Picking up two random books from the pile, I tugged Aaron's sleeve to tell him to follow.

Bleak House by Charles Dickens.

D.

Literature, on the first floor.

I don't know if it was the spiral staircase or the sound of Aaron's feet right behind me that made me dizzy. At the top, we disappeared between two narrow bookshelves. We were completely alone. My blush wrapped itself around my whole body and burned.

"You didn't call," he said.

"No," I whispered. "My sister broke her wrist so I've been a bit distracted."

"I forgive you," Aaron replied, glancing at *A Christmas Carol* on the shelf. "I'm going to see that in a few weeks. A musical version of *Scrooge* with my mum. She loves it. Dragging us all to the theater. Max isn't happy about it."

"I love Christmas," I said quickly, keen to move the conversation away from his brother. "Turkey and presents and all the buildup and stuff."

"What was your best one?" Aaron asked, putting his elbow on the shelf.

"Easy. One in France. I was about seven and I made this snowman out of—"

"Snow?" Aaron finished.

I pushed *Bleak House* into a gap. "Well, obviously. But also a croissant."

"Did you just say *croissant?*"

"Well, I didn't have a banana or anything else for its mouth so I had to make do with what I could find. I'm very resourceful," I told him.

"What did you call the snowman?" Aaron asked. "Pierre?"

"Fred, actually."

"Very French."

"He looked like a Fred!"

"How do Freds look?"

"Jolly," I said after a pause. "And old. We stuck a flat cap on the snowman's head and put a pipe in the croissant. A pretend one, anyway. Made out of a stick . . . What?" I asked because Aaron was staring at me with twinkling eyes.

"Nothing," he said in a way that told me it was something, and something good.

He moved his finger up and down the spines, and my own back tingled. I inched forward and Aaron did, too, and Stuart there was only one book between us now, but it just so happened to be the one on the Berlin Wall, which I'm sure you know was impossible to climb over. Aaron smiled and I smiled then our faces grew serious across the great expanse of that thirty-centimeter space. Blood pounding in my ears, I leaned closer and—

"Excuse me."

We spun around in unison to see an old lady in an anorak.

"I'm looking for a book for my granddaughter who's coming to stay. Could you recommend something?" Grimacing in frustration, I charged down the spiral steps to the Children's section and handed her the first thing I could find, a picture book called

Molly the Moo Cow. The old lady blinked. "My granddaughter's sixteen. And a vegetarian."

By the time I'd found a suitable book, Mrs. Simpson had appeared by the beanbags, dressed in a pale yellow cardigan with flowers for buttons.

"There's a lot of filing in the office, Zoe," she said, her neat bob like a helmet of hair around her pointy face.

"But I need to return this," I said, waving the book on the Berlin Wall. "And Literature's looking a bit messy." Mrs. Simpson followed my gaze. Aaron was still in the *D* section, waiting for me to return.

"I can do that," she sniffed. "You're needed in the back."

She stared at me until I moved. Faster even than the speed of light, I sorted the papers into piles, standing over a table, scared Aaron was going to leave without saying good-bye. The seventh time I looked through the glass in the door, that's precisely what had happened. His desk was empty. His bag was gone.

I sank onto a chair, but just as my bum hit the seat, there was a knock on the window, and Stuart I would love to pretend Aaron's hair was sticking up and there was a leaf dangling from his fringe to make it sound as if he'd climbed through hedges and all that to get to me. But that would be a lie, because he was just standing on an ordinary pavement as cars roared behind him, and there was nothing special about it whatsoever except my heart didn't seem to realize. It soared out of my chest and into the sky, a flash of scarlet in all the blue.

Aaron waved and I waved. He put his hand on the glass and I put mine on the glass and he did this joking face, making his eyes big and fluttering like we were having a special moment. And the funny thing was, we actually were, and we both knew it, which is why our cheeks burned the exact same color of brightest red.

From,

Zoe x

1 Fiction Road

Bath, UK

S. Harris #993765
Polunsky Unit (Death Row)
Livingston, Texas 77351
USA
December 25

Hey Stuart,

It's the first hour of Christmas Day and cold enough to see my breath so I'm very glad of the hat and scarf and Dad's jacket. I won't stay long because my fingers are already numb and no doubt Dot will be up at the crack of dawn to see if Santa's been, but I wanted you to know I'm thinking of you, hoping you're sleeping soundly in your cell like baby Jesus, except with a scar and a shaved head and no visitors bringing you gold, frankincense, or myrrh. Don't worry, you're not missing out on much, because I found out in Religious Education that myrrh is a sort of sticky tree resin. If you ask me, Wise Man Number Three was a bit mean to give oak goo to the Savior of the World. He would have been better off riding across the desert on his camel with something more traditional, e.g., chocolates in the shape of reindeer, which, by the way, you'll find in the bottom of your envelope.

Dot was hyper last night, cantering up and down the living room, her hands by her head in the manner of antlers. Her excitement made me ache. Maybe you ache, too, Stuart. Maybe you ache for the days you and your brother put a mince pie and a glass of sherry on the mantelpiece for Santa, because now you're in a cell and he's somewhere else far away, probably with a picture of your wife on his wall next to a bare Christmas tree that he hasn't the energy to decorate.

Anyway, I'm wasting time so I should make a start before Dot gets out of bed. Seeing as it's Christmas, I thought I'd tell

box of chocolates

you about last December so imagine the ground's frosty—the atmosphere in the study, too, because Dad had finally left his job and was filling in an application with Mum hovering over his shoulder.

"No apostrophe in *its*."

Dad tapped his fingers on the desk. "Yes, there is."

"Only when you mean *it is*. You don't need an apostrophe to show possession."

Dad pressed the DELETE button. "Why don't you apply for the job rather than correcting my application? It's your area of law."

Mum leaned forward to type. "We've talked about this. I'm not going through it all again." She picked up three used mugs and marched out of the room.

The house was cleaner than ever before, the taps gleaming in the bathroom and the furniture smelling of polish. Bedtimes were stricter and homework was checked more thoroughly and Mum made me redo a History essay to include all the facts I'd cut out about the Cold War, which was quite a lot because from what I can gather nothing much happened between Russia and America, like imagine a boxing match where two fighters just sit at opposite sides of the ring and flex their muscles without engaging in combat.

She made Dot practice her lip-reading, too, practically every day after school until Dad told her to give it a rest.

"How can I give it a rest when you won't give me any alternative?"

"Dot's exhausted," Dad said, and sure enough my sister had flopped over the side of the leather armchair, her arms dangling over her head. "Come on, Jane. That's enough for today."

"She's messing about," Mum said, yanking Dot back up to sitting.

"You've been at it for over an hour."

"One hour and twenty-two minutes," Soph muttered from the piano, crashing the keys in a minor chord and sounding so miserable that I grabbed her hand and pulled her upstairs into Mum and Dad's closet.

Mum's dresses swung from hangers as we scrambled among the shoes to get comfortable. I opened my pencil case and gave Soph my favorite fountain pen for a treat.

"What's up?" I asked in the darkness. It was a Friday night without much moon so the closet was that thick sort of black. I grabbed a crayon and inhaled deeply as Soph chewed on her lip. "Right, here's the deal. You tell me what's going on with you and I'll tell you what's going on with me."

She contemplated this for a second then blurted out, "They keep calling me names."

"Who do?"

"All the girls in my class. All of them. And tonight there's a sleepover with a Ouija board, and Portia's going to ask the ghost to reveal my secrets."

"Have you told a teacher?" She looked at me as if I was mental so I grabbed her hands, abandoning the crayon in Dad's shoe. "You have to tell someone." Soph screwed up her face. "You have to," I said more firmly. "Mum or Dad, if you don't want to say anything at school."

"Okay," she whispered, nodding slightly. "If it gets worse. Maybe Mum."

It was my turn to talk so I told her about Max.

"He keeps asking to meet by the lockers after school."

"Do you go?"

"It's Max Morgan, isn't it? You don't say no."

"What happens when you get there?"

I rolled my eyes. "What do you think, Soph?"

"So are you his girlfriend or what?" she asked, sucking on the end of the fountain pen.

"*Or what.* He hasn't asked me out or anything."

"So you just kiss and talk and—"

"We don't even talk. Just kiss. Not every day. When he feels like it. I think he fancies me, though."

"What about you? Do you fancy him?"

"Yeah, I do," I said, thinking of his dark brown hair and dark brown eyes and the lopsided smile that made the other girls jealous when it was directed straight at me.

"So why don't you ask him out?" she suggested, and I muttered something about Mum, but Stuart that wasn't the reason I was keeping my options open, and you know it.

Aaron had been to the library three times since the moment by the window. He'd write essays and I'd stack shelves, but as our bodies pretended to work, our eyes would do this secret dance. They'd flick together, then away. Together, then away. Together, hold, blink blink blinnnnnk . . . and then we'd smile

136

shyly, and the whole thing would start all over again. We'd talk, too, about everything and nothing, whispering between bookshelves and at his desk and once in the foyer when I was pinning up a poster about a reading group. I didn't ask about his girlfriend and Aaron didn't mention her. Honest truth, I had no idea where I stood, so I decided to let the situation play out for a while. To see what happened. No harm in that, I told myself. If nothing physical happened with Aaron and I didn't agree to anything exclusive with Max, I wasn't doing anything wrong.

My last shift before Christmas was on December 19. It had snowed heavily, fifteen centimeters in total, clean and white and fluffy, the sort of snow you'd make out of cotton wool on a card if you were trying to capture the perfect Christmas. Every time the revolving door spun, I looked up, smiling, but Aaron didn't walk in at 9 AM or 10 AM or 11 AM, and when he wasn't there at 12 PM, I slumped behind the computer, my Santa hat drooping as I typed numbers into a spreadsheet about borrowing figures.

"You can go," Mrs. Simpson said when the clock hit one.

"It's okay," I said, pretending to study the spreadsheet. "I'll just put a few more numbers in."

"I can finish that."

"No, really, I don't mind," I said, and if the mouse had been real, then Stuart, it would've squeaked because I was gripping it so hard. Mrs. Simpson put down her coffee then shooed me away.

"Go. Your dad will be waiting. Oh, and Zoe?" With a rare

smile, she pressed the badge pinned neatly to her cardigan. It flashed *Ho Ho Ho* as she waved.

The library was in the center of the city and the streets were crammed with Christmas shoppers and tourists. Sighing heavily, I wandered down to the pavement, annoyed Dad was late.

"Zoe?" came a voice from my right. "Zoe!"

Aaron was waving, standing in the middle of the library garden in a coat and mismatched gloves.

"You're here! I thought you weren't . . . Hi!" I exclaimed, unable to hide my delight.

Aaron beckoned me over. "Nice hat."

I nudged it so it flopped to the side at a jaunty angle, the pom-pom dangling by my chin. "Thanks."

"And it's appropriate attire for your surprise . . . Happy Christmas!" he said, pointing at something at his feet.

"Thanks," I said uncertainly, not sure what I was supposed to make of the snowball that came up to his waist.

"It was supposed to be bigger. And I couldn't find a flat cap or a pipe." He stared at me desperately. "It's Fred! Your French snowman, Fred." Aaron grabbed a croissant out of a plastic bag and stuck it in the middle of the snowball. "Voilà!"

I started to giggle. "But where's the head? And eyes? And nose?"

"I ran out of time," Aaron mumbled. The croissant fell off the snow and landed by our feet. "Oh God, it's pathetic, isn't it?"

"A little bit," I said, laughing, and then I stopped because Aaron was gazing at me, shaking his head.

"God, you have a sexy laugh." My face was cold and my toes were frozen, but inside I was warm warm warm warm warm. "Your giggle . . . right up there with my dad's sneeze and the squeak of green beans as my all-time favorite sounds."

"Your dad's sneeze?" I repeated, because I couldn't for the life of me think what else to say. He pretended to do it, loud on the *AAAAA* but ridiculously quiet and high on the *chooooooo*, and then held out his hands. I nodded in complete agreement. "That *is* a great noise."

"I heard it every night for years. We had this cat, you see. Ugly thing."

"Don't be mean!"

"You didn't see her! She was fat, really fat, and too furry, with a squashed-up face. I was devoted to her, though. So was my dad. I mean, he's allergic to cats, but he let her sit on his lap anyway, and he'd sneeze all evening. Mum would get on at him, calling him stupid and telling him to put the cat in the kitchen, but Dad said he loved the cat and the cat loved him, so he didn't mind. 'True love's about sacrifice.' That's what Dad said."

"Jesus, too."

"Yeah. But Jesus didn't bang the next-door neighbor, making anything he said about love totally irrelevant."

"He might have done," I muttered, surprised by the sudden bitterness in Aaron's tone. "I always get the feeling the Bible left out the juicy bits. Jesus was a man, wasn't he? He went to the bathroom. Burped." I wiggled my eyebrows. "Scratched himself down there when no one was looking. Maybe he had an affair."

"You," Aaron said, stepping over the croissant so he was standing directly in front of me, "are completely unique." I shook my head quickly. "You are, Zoe. A belching son of God? A blue furry creature called Bizzle?" he said, earning himself massive brownie points for remembering the name. "Who else imagines that stuff?"

"I dunno, but I reckon Jesus's burp would make my list of all-time favorite sounds."

Aaron laughed, his breath warm on my face. "What else would?"

I crinkled up my nose as I thought. "The noise of birds' wings when they take off. That's a cool sound."

"The sound of freedom."

"Precisely," I replied, amazed that he understood without me having to explain. "Oh, and you know what else?" I asked, but I never got the chance to describe the tap of Skull's claws on the kitchen tiles, because Aaron's phone had started to ring, a noise I didn't like one bit. We both stared down at the name on the screen.

ANNA

"I should go," I said suddenly.

"No. It's okay." His phone fell silent as he put it back in his pocket. "She can wait. But my mum can't," he said, sounding disappointed as he gazed over my shoulder. I turned to see a

140

plump woman with black hair and mahogany highlights hurrying toward the library, studying us closely. "I said I'd give her a lift back home."

"No worries. My dad will be here in a minute, anyway."

He bent down to pick up the croissant and stuck it back on the snowman, where it stayed in place. "S'long, Bird Girl."

"S'long," I said, grinning as he ran off to meet his mum, his words ringing in my ears. *She can wait.*

Well, after that, of course I couldn't resist sending him a message, though I managed to hold off until the evening so as not to look too keen.

Thanks again for my surprise. Fred was without doubt the best non-snowman the world has ever seen.

I don't know about that, he replied straightaway. Have you seen The Snowman? The little boy waking up to the pile of snow at the end? Surely that's the best non-snowman.

No way! He was all drippy and dead. A pile of slush. Fred is better.

Fred appreciates your kind words, but he knows he can't compete with a snowman that FLEW TO THE SOUTH POLE.

You mean the North Pole?!

Whatever. Wherever. HE FLEW. IN THE SKY.

But Fred's smile is made out of pastry. That has to count for something. . . .

The conversation was still going on when I stumbled outside in my wellies to fill up the bird feeder, ready for the morning. My phone vibrated against my thigh as I poured seeds into the wire mesh tube. Smiling, I pulled it out of my pocket.

Missing ur kisses ha x

My face fell. Max. I jumped as the phone beeped again.

It counts for a lot, I'll give you that. Sweet dreams, Bird Girl. p.s. Fred says bonne nuit out of the corner of his croissant x

I laughed. I couldn't help it, even though my mind was conjuring up a picture of two brothers, side by side in the same room with their phones, no idea they were texting the same girl. The bird feeder swung from the branch as I gazed up at the stars. Aaron liked me. And I liked him. Girlfriend or no girlfriend, I wasn't being fair to Max. I decided to cool things off with him over the next few days and put a stop to it after Christmas.

Surprise surprise, Mum and Dad spent the whole of it arguing.

"How do you know where those birds have been kept? They might just write *free-range* on the packet so mugs like us pay twice as much."

"If it says *free-range*, then it's free-range," Mum replied, tossing some carrots into the supermarket trolley and wandering forward. "There are laws for these things, as you should know. Didn't you used to be a lawyer?"

"Didn't you, too?" Dad replied as I trailed behind, sick to death of it. I looked at Dad's crossed arms and Mum's hands gripping the cart, neither of them willing to concede, and Stuart honest truth it felt as if the Cold War was still going on right here in the supermarket by the potatoes in the vegetable aisle.

"Look, there's no point in spending all that money on a turkey when money's tight," Dad said.

"It's only tight because you can't get a—" Mum stopped herself at the last moment, picking up a bag of sprouts.

"Go on," Dad growled. "*Say it.* I dare you."

"Do you think there are enough in here?" Mum asked, weighing the bag in her hand.

In the end, Mum got her own way about the turkey, and despite everything it was golden and delicious and smelled beautiful on Christmas morning, cooking in the oven as we exchanged presents. For once, Grandpa had sent us something, cards with money inside them, though they were written in Dad's handwriting. He beamed as Soph tucked the twenty-pound note into the waistband of her pajama bottoms. Dad asked Mum if it would be okay for us to visit the hospital, maybe the following day, but she just sprayed her new perfume hard, making us all cough.

"Santa's rubbish," Dot said when Mum and Dad left the

living room to make the stuffing. She was signing more easily because her cast had been removed. "He didn't even *read* my list."

"What did you ask for?"

"An iPod."

"But you can't hear music."

"Or a phone, so I can get an upgrade." She held up a broken calculator and pressed the buttons sadly.

By the evening she'd cheered up, sprinting into my room with no clothes on to ask if I wanted to smell her new bubble bath. As I picked her up and plunked her in the water, I sniffed the air.

"Oranges?" I signed. "Or peach? Or strawberries and bananas and kiwis all mixed together?" I joked as Soph grimaced.

She was sitting with her back against the radiator, trying to encourage Skull to tackle a jump she'd made out of a bottle of dandruff shampoo and two bars of soap. Sloshing about in the water, Dot told me about a project on the future that she was starting at school, and how her class was going to make a time capsule, putting all sorts of stuff into a box then bury it underground.

"I'm going to put in one thing, and that is a dandelion."

"A dandelion?"

"To show the aliens in one hundred years what flowers we have now," Dot explained. Soph grinned, and I did, too, and Dot beamed in the bubbles, but I don't think she understood what was funny.

"The dandelion will be dead in one hundred years," Soph said out loud.

"Shhh!" I warned, but Soph just smirked.

"Dot, the dandelion will rot," she signed clearly. Dot's brow crumpled.

"Not if you bury it carefully," I signed, glaring at Soph, who stuck out her tongue. "It will be fine."

"Do you think the aliens will like it?" Dot asked.

I lifted her out of the water and wrapped her in a towel. "They'll love it."

When she was dry, I put her to bed, trying to ignore Mum and Dad bickering downstairs about who was going to do the washing up. Snuggled up under her duvet, I signed a story about a little green man who lived in the traffic lights. When I got to the end, she asked me to sign it again.

"Greedy!" I said, tickling her sides.

"Well, do you want your Christmas present instead?" she asked. Before I could answer, her chubby knees hit the carpet and she grabbed a package wrapped in a plastic bag from underneath her bed.

"A book!"

"That's not the present," Dot replied, opening the front cover carefully. "Flowers don't rot, Zoe. *Look*." In between the first two pages was a squashed, dried dandelion. "You said they were your favorite that day in the garden."

"They *are* my favorite," I said, and Stuart it wasn't a lie, because all of a sudden they were.

"Merry Christmas," she signed.

"Merry Christmas," I whispered, and Stuart it's time for me to go, so a very Merry Christmas to you, too.

Love from,
Zoe x
1 Fiction Road
Bath, UK

S. Harris #993765
Polunsky Unit (Death Row)
Livingston, Texas 77351
USA
January 1

Hey Stuart,

Well, I was going to hold up my glass of water and say cheers and wish you a Happy New Year and all that, but perhaps that's not the right thing to do. Probably prison inmates don't wait up until midnight like the rest of the world, because there's nothing to celebrate. Normally on December 31, people are thinking about the good things they've done in the past year and the fun they've got to look forward to in the next, e.g., leaving school or learning to drive or going to college or whatever. Prisoners don't have anything to get excited about, from what I can gather, unless people on Death Row cheer on the stroke of midnight because they're one step closer to execution. Or maybe they're waving their arms in the air as they've got one more year under their belt, a year they didn't think they'd have. Perhaps living in something the size of this shed is better than not living at all.

Stuart, that's so sad and sort of reminds me of *A Christmas Carol*, to be honest. If you've never read Dickens or seen *The Muppets* then let me explain that Bob Cratchit was a very poor man so his family could only afford the tiniest Victorian goose on December 25. His children still gazed at it as if it was a great big bird with thick white flesh that would feed them for weeks, clapping when it was put on the table. Their applause seemed a bit over-the-top for what they were actually getting, and that is exactly the same as you in an orange jumpsuit, holding your own hand while singing "Auld Lang Syne," celebrating the tiny bit of life you can live in your cell.

In case you're wondering, *Auld Lang Syne* is Scottish for "Old Times' Sake," according to my Geography teacher. We sing it to remember the good times we've had with the people from our past, which is a whole lot nicer than my original interpretation. Lauren told me the correct words twelve months ago, and I think that's where we'll begin tonight, with her laughing her head off when she realized I'd misheard the lyrics and thought everyone celebrated the end of the year by singing about a pensioner's dodgy vision.

"Old Lan's eye! As if you believed it was that!"

"Shut up," I said, whacking her with a balloon because we were getting stuff ready for her party. Lauren had only decided to invite people around that morning when her mum had announced that her boyfriend had booked a surprise trip to London for a long weekend. "A dirty one," she'd explained on the phone. "They're going to F in the Hilton."

I blew up a balloon.

"How many people are coming tonight?"

Lauren took the balloon out of my hand, tied a knot in the bottom, and hit it into a growing pile.

"No idea. Invited everyone I know, though, so hopefully enough people will turn up. My brother asked a few of his friends, too." She poked me in the ribs. "Max said he's coming." When I didn't reply, she said, "You're excited, aren't you?"

"Yeah. Yeah, 'course I am," I said, forcing a grin, though I was thinking about the dozens of messages he'd sent over Christmas and how I'd only replied to a few. Enough to be polite, though it must have been obvious that I was losing interest.

"Good! Because if you don't want him, I'll have him. Seriously. Last term I heard these girls talking about you in the bathroom and they were all like 'Oh God, she's so lucky!' Then that Becky with the weird neck said she's had a crush on him for three years, not that she's got any chance unless Max has a weird fetish for swans." I smiled properly this time. "Right, that's done," Lauren said when the last balloon had been blown up and dropped onto the pile. "You can go in the shower first. Time to get yourself ready for lover boy."

Now Stuart you're probably surprised that I was allowed to go to this party, but Mum had only agreed because I'd said we were having a girls' night in.

"A girls' night in? Doing what?"

"Painting our nails. Watching a movie," I'd replied, and in case you're wondering, I felt no guilt whatsoever about lying after all her Christmas arguments with Dad.

"Keep your nails subtle," she'd said. "You've got school in a couple of days. And don't watch anything unsuitable, my love. No horror or anything. I've got that cartoon of the giant if you want it?"

A few hours later, *Shrek* lay abandoned on Lauren's bed and the house was packed, and I mean packed, like one of the suitcases I take on holiday with the zip almost bursting because I just can't travel light. I joined the crowd around the drinks table in the kitchen, weaving my hand through five bodies to take a handful of chips and a bottle of wine. Mum popped into my head as I popped the cork, but I poured myself a large glass, and honest truth it looked great in my hand, the wine and my nails an identical shade of red.

Music kicked in and people started to dance wherever they were, in the hall or the porch or the living room, moving in time to the thumping beats, drinks splashing out of plastic cups and also mugs and even a milk jug because Lauren had run out of glasses. Hips thrust and shoulders jerked and heads swayed, everyone in the house moving as one, and for the first time ever

I was right in the middle of it, all *Wooooo* and waving my arms in the center of the kitchen near the toaster.

Funny how clever your eyes can be, how they can spot things in your sideways vision when you're staring at something directly in front of you. Lauren was twirling under my arm in a sparkly top, but out of the corner of my eye I saw a black jacket and red hair, flames on coal flickering faintly on my radar. My stomach lurched with recognition, and sure enough, Anna walked into the kitchen with Aaron right behind in an oversize sweater. Lauren's brother must have invited him—that was the only explanation—and I forgot to dance and just stared and stared. After all the flirting. The *snowman*. My fists clenched as Aaron laughed at something the girl whispered in his ear. Gutted, I watched him touch her arm and ask if she wanted a drink, pointing at the table full of beer and wine and vodka just to my right.

NO!

I don't know if I said that out loud or in my head as the girl nodded and Aaron started to move in my direction. My first instinct was to hide, but where? Behind the armchair in the far corner? The cupboards, jumping in next to the cereal? Panicking, I ducked behind a tall boy with acne as Aaron pushed past Lauren. My pulse quickened. He reached the drinks table. My pulse raced. He nodded at the boy with spots. My pulse exploded. One meter away—that's all he was, and I couldn't let him see me, not if he was here with another girl and his brother was probably somewhere in the house, too.

Cringing, I turned away from the drinks table, determined to

151

stare in the opposite direction until he'd gone, but as that man Orpheus realized in the underworld, that's a whole lot easier than it sounds. FYI Orpheus is someone from Greek mythology and to rescue his wife he had to lead her out of danger without looking back to see her face. Just as he was about to succeed, he glanced over his shoulder, and his wife vanished into thin air. Unfortunately, when I looked at Aaron, he didn't disappear into thin air or fat air or any sort of air for that matter. Instead, he ate a nacho, so close I could almost hear the crunch.

He grabbed two beers, swinging them in his hand as he returned to the girl. Standing on tiptoe, I saw him stroke her back to announce his presence, all his DNA sparkling between her shoulder blades. Tears filled my eyes. Lowering my head, I pushed through the crowd, out of the kitchen, and into the hall, desperate to get away, but someone grabbed my hand as I started on the stairs.

I followed the fingers to the palm. The palm to the wrist. The wrist to the arm, my heart beating faster and faster only to stop dead as I realized the hand belonged to Max and not his brother. He was stretching, straining to maintain contact, and his face came in and out of view as people pushed up and down the stairs. He was shouting something I couldn't hear as his fingers tightened around my wrist and pulled. I resisted at first. He pulled harder, tugging me down the stairs toward him. Toward Aaron. Wine splashed out of my glass as I slipped.

"Outside," Max mouthed.

His grip was firm. We moved down the hall and I kept my eyes on the carpet, terrified of being seen. When the front door came into view, I made it easier for Max, speeding up and walking with more purpose because Stuart I wanted to disappear. Stepping over legs, we turned sideways to squeeze through small gaps between people, the music getting louder and the hall getting hotter and our feet getting slower as we tried to push our way to the porch.

At last, Max's fingers touched the brass handle. He tugged hard then tugged me, too, pulling me into the garden. Snow crunched under our feet and icicles sparkled on windowsills and bare branches made black lines against the orange of the streetlights. Max led me behind a fir tree, and the house disappeared from view.

"It's crazy in there," I said, my voice strangely flat.

"But nice out here," Max replied, handing me his jacket. "Here. Put that on." Shoving my arms into the coat, wine spilled out of my glass, splattering the frozen ground. "It's good to see you."

"You, too," I said, because Stuart it sort of was. He smiled as if relieved then pulled me between his legs. I put my glass on the wall then linked my hands behind his neck. "Good Christmas?"

"Boring," Max muttered, going straight in for the kiss, and his lips were soft and familiar and comforting.

Somewhere to my right, there was a cough. I jerked away, scared it was Aaron, but a man rounded the corner, walking his dog.

The front door creaked. I jumped again. Moving the branches of the fir tree to one side, I strained to see, but it was just a girl lighting a cigarette.

Max rubbed my arm. "You're a bit twitchy."

I swallowed then said, "Shouldn't we go somewhere a bit more private?"

Max smirked then kissed the tip of my cold nose. "What do you have in mind?"

I moved my face to one side, but Max's lips brushed my neck as he put his hands on my bum. "It just feels a bit open. And I'm freezing."

Max thought for a moment. "Wait here," he said, running off before I could protest.

He was back a couple of minutes later, something silver jangling in his hand. He waved the keys in the air.

"My brother's car's parked down the road."

My mouth fell open. "We can't do that!"

"Relax. My brother's cool. I asked him," Max said, starting to walk.

I stayed where I was, my heart thumping in my chest. "You *asked* him? What did you say?"

Max turned around and walked backward, beckoning me with his finger. "I said I had a girl and we were looking for somewhere warm. 'Just to talk,' I told him, but my brother laughed like he knew exactly what I had in mind."

I chased after Max, frantic now. "Did you say who I was? Did you mention my name?"

Max opened his lips to reply, and then paused. "Why?"

It took a lot of effort, but I managed to relax my voice. "Just . . . well, I don't want to get a reputation. Not after the whole photo thing."

Max put his hand on my back and moved me gently toward the car. DOR1S appeared at the end of the street. I thought of the dice hanging off the mirror. Miss Scarlet.

"Maybe we should go back to the party," I said.

Max applied more pressure to my back. "Relax. There's nothing to worry about. I didn't tell my brother your name."

"Still. I don't think this is a good idea."

Max sighed in frustration. "Why not?"

"Well, it's just that . . . I don't know . . . It just feels a bit . . ."

"Come on, Zoe," Max said, sounding annoyed, and there was nothing gentle about his push now. "I haven't seen you all Christmas, and I'm—"

"You're *what*, exactly?" I said, jamming my feet into the pavement so he couldn't pull me any farther.

"*You know*," he said, trying to be all cheeky about it. "And I know you want to," he whispered in my ear.

"Let's go back to the house," I pleaded. When Max frowned, I added, "Find an empty room." I took a step closer and lowered my voice, hating myself but forcing out the words, anything to get away from Aaron's car. "An empty room with a bed."

The keys disappeared into the pocket of Max's jeans. "Now you're talking."

We started to walk.

There was the wall. And the tree. And the girl smoking a cigarette.

There was the drive. And the door. And the house heaving with people, impossible to make out in the darkness. Aaron could have been anywhere.

But he wasn't anywhere, Stuart. He was right there in front of us, standing in the doorway, facing into the house. My eyes widened in horror as I stared at the back of his head. Max pointed.

"That's my brother. Over there."

"Let's go the other way!" I squeaked. Without waiting for his reply, I yanked Max across the garden. He filled his lungs and opened his mouth, and I realized with a great thrill of fear that he was going to shout.

"Aaron!"

I dropped Max's hand just as Aaron started to turn. An ear came into view. A nose. With a leap, I sprang two meters to my right, then dashed into the shadows.

"Back already?" Aaron said. Something jangled through the air—the car keys being thrown.

"We changed our minds."

"We?" Aaron asked, and I imagined his head moving from side to side as he searched for another person. I told myself not to look, but my neck twisted and my head turned and this time when I saw Aaron, I wished with all my heart that there really was an underworld that could suck Aaron into darkness.

His eyes narrowed and his neck strained as he leaned forward to make out the girl in the shadows, wrapped in his brother's jacket.

"Aaron, this is Zoe," Max said.

"Zoe?" Aaron repeated, and something in his voice made my insides hurt. I stepped out of the shadows, because Stuart the game was up. "Zoe," Aaron said again. "You're with my brother?"

"Just tonight," I said quickly.

Max put his arm around my shoulder. "Well, and all the other times before."

"Other times? Like when?" Aaron seemed to realize this question might sound odd and forced a smile. "How long have you been keeping her quiet, Max?"

"Not long," he said, enjoying the attention. "Only since September."

"September?"

Max misinterpreted the reason for his brother's surprise. "Hey, everyone's got secrets. You don't breathe a word about your—"

"Because there's nothing to tell," Aaron replied. I drew myself up a little taller. I might not have been innocent, but Aaron wasn't, either.

"What about—" I was about to say *Anna* but realized it might look suspicious.

"What about what?"

"Your girlfriend," I muttered, pointing back into the house. "The one with red hair."

157

"Anna?" Max said, sounding surprised. "Is that who you mean?"

"We're just friends," Aaron replied, and my stomach dropped. "Known her since I was four."

"But . . . but I saw you together. At the bonfire," I spluttered. "You were hugging and she—"

"Had just broken up with her boyfriend," Aaron finished. "I was looking after her. She's like a sister or cousin or something."

"Right," I said, and I was surprised how normally the sound came out when everything inside me was screaming.

"Not like you two," Aaron said, walking into the garden, his hands in his pockets. "Why did you keep her a secret, Max? Have you gone all shy or something?" His tone was jokey, and Max laughed.

"Whatever. She's been to the house. Not my fault you weren't there."

I closed my eyes.

"What?" Aaron said, his mouth tightening even though his tone was light. "When?"

"I dunno, like November or something. You came over for a bit, didn't you?"

I opened my eyes slowly.

"Yeah. Yeah, I did."

The wind picked up, blowing Max's coat around my body. Even though I was freezing, I wanted to tear it off and throw it to the ground.

"Let's go inside," Max said, taking my hand.

"Actually," I replied, dropping his fingers, "I don't feel that well. I think I'm just going to go home." I took off his jacket. "I need to lie down. *Alone*," I added, because Max had winked.

Without looking at either of the brothers, I set off across the grass, desperate to call Dad to ask for an early lift. Max shouted after me.

"What about your coat and stuff?"

I stopped and swore under my breath. "Damn it. They're in Lauren's room. Could you get them for me?" Max didn't look that pleased, but he disappeared into the house, leaving me and Aaron alone.

Neither of us spoke.

I wondered if his heart was thumping like mine.

"I'm sorry," I said at last. "I should've said."

Aaron sniffed. "No apology needed. Nothing happened between us."

I swallowed. Paused. Flexed my fingers. "There was something. . . ."

Aaron looked surprised. "Was there?"

Stepping forward, I muttered, "You know there was."

Aaron crossed his arms. "You're just a girl I keep bumping into. Someone I barely know."

The words hit me in the pit of my stomach. "You don't mean that."

He nodded too long. "I do. You and my brother, you make a good couple."

"We're not a couple."

"Doesn't look that way from where I'm standing."

I brushed my hair out of my eyes. "I'm sorry, okay?"

Aaron kept his voice cool in his reply. "Like I said, no apology needed. You're free to see whoever you want. Why wouldn't you be?"

"Because we're—"

"*Friends*," Aaron finished. "If that. Acquaintances more than anything."

"Fine!"

"It *is* fine," Aaron said, all condescending as if I was acting crazy or something. I glared at him, and Stuart maybe I had no right to be furious, but try telling that to the anger thundering through my veins.

"If that's how you want it!"

"That's how it is," Aaron replied in the same cool tone. He smiled, but it didn't reach his eyes. "Have fun with my brother," he said before walking back into the party, and as I watched him leave, I decided right there and then that fun with Max was precisely what I was going to have.

The first morning of the year began with a bright red sunrise as if all my anger was burning in the sky. After Dad had picked me up, agreeing not to say anything about the party to Mum, I'd barely slept, just tossed and turned the conversation in my mind until I couldn't remember what Aaron had said or what I'd said, but I knew that he was In The Wrong, and Stuart I've done those capitals on purpose to show you how convinced I was of this Concrete Fact.

I smashed open the fridge door and poured milk too roughly,

planning my revenge. I'd make Max fall in love with me and maybe I'd fall in love with him, too, and we'd walk up mountains and sit at the top in the fog and it would serve Aaron right. I chucked the spoon into the sink, where it clattered against a bowl.

"Happy New Year to you, too," Soph said, her mouth full of cereal.

"Manners, Sophie," Mum snapped, looking up from the laptop.

Only Dot was in a good mood, prancing around with a list of resolutions tucked into her pajama bottoms.

"So, my first is to go on a diet," she signed, pointing at her plump belly. "My second is to learn to fly by watching the birds, and my third is to be kind to everyone except teachers and strangers who might want to steal me, and my fourth is to . . ." She went on and on, then scrambled onto my knee, asking about my resolutions.

"Don't have any."

"How about *To work hard and do well in my exams at the end of the year*?" Mum chipped in, her eyes glued to a website about cochlear implants.

"They're only mocks."

"Mocks are important, Zoe. If you're going into law, then—"

"Who says I'm going into law?" I muttered.

Mum typed something quickly. "Well, what are you going to do instead?"

"Maybe write. Maybe not. I don't know yet. I don't need a plan."

"That's ridiculous." Mum sighed, clicking a couple of buttons.

"No, it's not." I sulked. "There's no rush, is there? I'll just see how I feel when I finish school." Mum tutted at me so I tutted right back, and I was sent upstairs for being cheeky.

I slumped at my desk, waiting for Aaron to apologize. Now Stuart I don't know when cell phones were invented, if it was before or after your murder trial, so maybe you've never been in the position of waiting hours for a message. If so, trust me, that's one thing you should be grateful for, because it's torture hearing imaginary beeps, your hopes rising rising rising as you check your phone, only to have your heart crash back down, shattering on the empty screen.

So yeah, time definitely dragged that day, and the TV didn't help. There was nothing on but back-to-back old films. I'm sure you've heard of *Gone with the Wind*, and who knows, maybe you've even seen it, and if so I'm wondering if you managed to stay awake, because that film is long—so long I had to go to the bathroom twice before it finished. When I got fidgety on the sofa, Mum kept whispering "Just be patient!" as though there was going to be this great reward for the effort I was putting in. I watched all four hours waiting to see the lovers get together at the end, so you can imagine my disappointment when the man called Rhett walked out on the woman called Scarlett just before the final credits. I looked at Mum like *That surely can't be it*, but Rhett didn't come back and Scarlett didn't run after him, so that was how the film ended.

Gone with the Wind was an even bigger disappointment than *The Great Escape* (they don't escape) so I grabbed the remote out of Mum's hand and bashed the OFF button.

"Didn't you like it? It's one of the greatest love stories ever told," Mum said.

"Well, that's depressing."

"Less depressing than *Titanic*," Soph yawned. "At least Rhett didn't freeze to death then sink to the bottom of the ocean."

The door burst open and Dot ran in carrying Skull. She dropped onto her knees with the rabbit's ears poking up over her shoulder.

"Is that wind thing over?" she managed to sign.

"*Gone with the Wind*," Mum corrected her.

"I know why it's called that." Dot smirked, and I could tell she'd been practicing a joke.

Mum thought hard. "I think it refers to Rhett leaving at the end, as if he's blown away by the wind," she signed seriously.

Dot shook her head, grinning from ear to ear. "It's because the man poops before he leaves the town."

That night I lay under my duvet, cross and miserable. Reaching out to my bedside table, I hit my phone one last time. It glowed green and blank. In the emerald light, I made shadow puppets on the wall. A dog barked near my bookshelf as a cat scrambled toward it, and even though dogs and cats don't usually get on, the ones in my room defied all the odds to curl up together on top of a dictionary. I watched them for a moment before rolling over, yearning for Aaron so much it hurt to be in my own skin. The window rattled as the wind blustered, and Stuart I got the strongest sense that he was being blown away.

Love from,

Zoe x

1 Fiction Road

Bath, UK

S. Harris #993765
Polunsky Unit (Death Row)
Livingston, Texas 77351
USA
January 22

Hey Stuart,

I've just heard the news. It was announced a couple of days ago, but I only went on the computer this evening. Most times when I click on the Internet, I type in your name to check for updates, and today there was a brand-new story in the *Houston Chronicle* that said your execution date has been set for May 1.

May 1, Stuart. I can't believe it. Of all the days.

My hands are shaking so it's difficult to write even though I'm quite comfy in a brand-new deck chair that Dad must've bought in a garden center sale or something. I can't imagine how you must be feeling. By my calculation, you're probably just having dinner, and I bet you anything you've lost your appetite. Of course, it goes without saying that I'll do everything I can to help. Maybe I could get in touch with the nun who came into school to talk about capital punishment and we can organize something, e.g., a protest or a petition signed by all the nuns in the convent.

The Texas government can't put you to sleep. They just can't. Only last week I read your poem "Forgiveness" and how you "Regret taking a life/With a carving knife/Especially your wife." Honest truth, I think you deserve a chance to redeem yourself. If I was the president of the United States, of course I would still have prisons, but they would help criminals rather than kill them as if there's no hope left. If you ask me, no one can write off a human like that, as if they've looked inside their soul and decided it's bad, all bad, without even the tiniest bit of good worth saving.

The least I can do is finish what I started. Now that we're running out of time, I have to be quick about it. I need to get to the end of my story before May 1, and I hope it takes your mind off the final preparations such as your last meal, which I imagine will be a cheeseburger with curly fries and a milk shake with two straws and a ketchup packet to remind you of the good times. Anyway let's get on, because we're working against the clock, so picture the big hand whizzing back twelve months to last January, and we'll start with me and Lauren sitting on a step outside school, shivering in our coats at break time on the first day of term.

"So, how was the rest of the party?" I asked.

Lauren locked her fingers together then blew into the hole. "Good. Brilliant, actually. Max missed you, though. He walked around with a face like a bear's backside after you'd gone. Even said no when Marie tried to hook up with him."

"What?" I said sharply.

"Don't worry, he didn't do anything. She just tried it on. Honestly, she was a real mess. Stumbling about, no clue what she was doing. She was sick all over my drive, and the next morning I saw a blackbird *eat* it."

"How did it happen?"

"It just sort of flew down and started to peck at the corner of—"

"No," I interrupted. "How did Max say no?"

Lauren explained how Marie had staggered up to him and gone in for the kiss, but he'd turned his head away, probably thinking of me.

"Either that or she stank of vomit," Lauren finished. "Either way. I think he likes you."

My depression since the party lifted a bit. So what if Aaron had said those things? His brother was interested, and I wanted to keep it that way, which is why I dashed out of French at the end of the day, running down some steps to the drama department, where I knew Max had his last class. He was coming out of the studio, shoveling chips into his mouth. I waved to get his attention, and he followed me around the corner.

"You okay?" Max asked.

"Great. Very happy. Not to be back at school. But you know. To see you."

Max grinned, wiping chips off his chin. "Me, too. Missed you at the party, Zo."

"Sorry I disappeared." I put my fingers on his belt. "Just when things were starting to get interesting . . ." I fiddled with his buckle. "It's a shame we didn't find that empty room." I tugged the end of his tie, feeling reckless, not like myself at all. "So . . . do you want to do something after school this week? I could come to your place?"

Max blinked in surprise and spoke in a strangled sort of voice. "Yeah, all right. If you like."

"I do like. Tuesday?"

"I see my dad on Tuesdays. How about Thursday?"

Something Lauren said in November came back to me. *It's a slippery slope*, and Stuart there I was choosing to plunge right down it. I stepped forward and kissed his cheek. "Perfect."

Mum dropped me off at Lauren's on Thursday night because I told her we had to finish the project on rivers.

"It's dragging on a bit, isn't it?"

"The Nile's long," I said coolly before climbing out of the car.

Looking back on it now, I can't believe I was so calm about it, turning away from Lauren's house when Mum had driven off, striding across the zebra crossing and hurrying through the green glow of the dragon in the Chinese takeout without even putting up a hood. Don't get me wrong—doubt flickered in my stomach as I stood outside Max's front door. Aaron's front door. But it wasn't enough to make me turn around. Aaron had told me I was free to see whoever I wanted. He'd said to have fun with his brother. I pulled myself up to my full height and knocked twice on the wood.

Keys tinkled. Hinges creaked. I wet my lips and fixed a smile on my face. A shaft of light spilled onto the garden path, and I was standing in the middle of the beam, facing a blond girl of about nine dressed in dungarees. A camera hung around her neck.

"Who are you?" she asked before I could speak.

"I'm Zoe. Who are you?"

"Fiona."

"Nice to meet—"

"Are you here to see Aaron or Max?"

Good question. "Max. If he's in?"

The girl spun around and charged up the stairs, leaving the front door open. I hesitated, seeing two pairs of boys' sneakers on the mat, but forced myself to step over them into the warmth of the house. A TV blared in the kitchen, the smell of melted cheese and garlic in the air. Glasses clinked and plates banged. Someone was cooking.

"Hello?" I called, feeling awkward.

"You must be Zoe," a voice said, and a plump face appeared around the kitchen door. Her black and reddish hair was tied back in a ponytail. Sandra smiled, but then her eyes narrowed. "Have we met before?"

"No," I said quickly, though with a jolt of alarm I realized she'd seen me outside the library. By the snowman. With Aaron.

"You sure? You look familiar."

"Well, we sort of have," I said in a casual voice. "I came over in November to see Max, but we never actually—"

"That must be it! Come on through." I followed her into the kitchen. "Lemonade okay?" she asked, pouring before I answered and shouting at the top of her voice. "*Max!* Take a seat, sweetheart. He'll be down in a minute."

I did as I was told, perching awkwardly at the small table in the corner of the kitchen, pretending to take an interest in the talk show on TV. The presenter had one of those cooked-sausage-skin faces, tanned and wrinkled, and he was announcing it was time for the lie-detector test.

"This is my favorite bit," Sandra muttered. "Pizza okay?"

"Great."

"They're in the oven. I've done some salad as well." She wiggled a plastic bag full of lettuce and shredded carrots and some purplish stuff that could have been beetroot. "Well, the shop's done it for me. We're eating *à la supermarché* this evening." It was supposed to be a joke so I forced a laugh as Sandra emptied the salad into a silver bowl and put it on the table. "That should be enough for five of us."

Me. Sandra. Max. Fiona. And Aaron.

My legs tensed under the table, my knees squeezing together. This was going to happen. This was actually going to happen. I was going to go through with it.

"Max only told me you were coming about two seconds ago, so it'll have to do, I'm afraid. Still. Everyone likes pizza, don't they?"

I tuned back into the conversation. "Yes. Yes, they do."

"Max!" Sandra shouted again, grabbing five sets of cutlery. "Fiona! Aaron! *Dinner's ready.*"

Somewhere upstairs, a floorboard squeaked. Two brothers got off their beds. Two pairs of feet hit the carpet.

There was a sound behind me. I braced myself, but it was Fiona. She scampered to a chair, then poured herself some orange juice and stared at me across the table.

More footsteps in the hall. Heavier ones. Two pairs.

I turned around and there they were. There *he* was, because Stuart I had eyes only for Aaron, beautiful in a plain T-shirt and gray jeans, his toes long and straight on the carpet. His jaw dropped as I boldly held his gaze. Something throbbed in the air between us.

"Kiss her," Fiona said, giggling suddenly as Max entered the kitchen.

"*Fiona,*" Sandra warned.

Max squeezed my shoulder and sat down on my right, leaving an empty space on my left. "I told Mum we didn't want any food."

"It's okay," I said as Aaron recovered from the shock.

"It's not," Max muttered. "Embarrassing."

Touching his thigh, I breathed, "Don't worry."

"Ooooh, whisper whisper," Fiona said. She picked a lettuce leaf out of the bowl and threw it in her mouth. "Lovey dovey. Kissy kissy."

Aaron grabbed a glass out of a cupboard and turned on the tap too hard. Water splashed everywhere, drenching his T-shirt.

Max laughed as Aaron flushed and dried himself with a tea towel. Almost in slow motion, he looked from the sink to the table, glancing from the seat next to me to the seat next to his sister. Rubbing his nose, he walked all the way around to the space by Fiona.

Sandra put the pizzas by the salad. The heat misted up the silver bowl. Fiona drew a heart in the steam and beamed in my direction.

"Pepperoni. Ham and pineapple. Margherita. There's half a pizza each, so choose wisely," Sandra said.

"*Mine*," Fiona said, snatching the margherita. Max picked up half the pepperoni. Sandra went for the ham and pineapple. I leaned forward as Aaron leaned forward. Both our hands reached for the margherita, and the pizza hung in the air between us.

"You have it," he said, dropping the crust.

"Do you want to share?"

Aaron stared straight into my eyes for the first time that evening. "No."

Fiona fiddled with her camera as she ate, tilting the screen toward Sandra.

"Here's one I took yesterday. And here's a picture of the grass that I took before school. *Look*," she said because Sandra was gawping at the talk show. "The drops of water are sparkling because of the sun."

"Lovely," Sandra said. "Christmas present," she explained to me. "She's a budding photographer."

"*Cheese!*" Fiona shouted suddenly, pointing the camera at my face. The flash exploded before I had a chance to pose. "That's really bad." She giggled, clicking a button and showing Aaron.

"Really bad," he agreed.

"Give her a chance to smile," Max said, picking up a piece of pepperoni and flinging it into his mouth. "Do another one." He put his arm around me and grinned at the camera. I had no choice but to grin, too, my hands in a knot and my lips stiff as Aaron looked away.

Silence fell as everyone went back to eating. There was just the sound of teeth and hard crusts and squelchy cheese. It was a relief when the talk-show host brought on the first guest to fail the lie-detector test. The crowd was on their feet, booing.

"Why are they doing that?" Fiona asked.

"He's a cheat," Sandra explained, transfixed by the screen. "Like most bloody men."

"What did he cheat in?"

"On," Aaron corrected her. "And it's who. *Who* did he cheat *on*?"

I swallowed my last mouthful of pizza with difficulty.

"So who did he cheat on?" Fiona prompted, circling her finger around her plate to pick up crumbs.

"His girlfriend," Aaron said.

"What did he do?" she asked.

Aaron put down his knife and fork, and Stuart they were pointing directly at me. "Kissed someone else."

"Shagged her, more like," Max said.

Fiona started to giggle. "*Shagged*," she repeated.

"Thank you, Max." Sandra sighed. "She's only nine."

Aaron stood up suddenly. He picked up his plate and Fiona's plate and Sandra's plate, taking them to the dishwasher. Sandra poured herself a large glass of wine.

"Pudding, anyone? Cup of tea?"

Max patted his stomach to say he was full. "Me and Zoe are going upstairs."

"To *sh*——" Fiona started.

"That's enough," Sandra snapped.

"Thanks for dinner, Mum," Aaron said, marching out of the kitchen without looking back.

"No worries, sweetheart," she called. "Good luck with your studying. He's got an exam tomorrow," Sandra told me. "History. He's a pretty smart boy."

"Yeah," Max said, a mix of pride and envy in his voice. "He got the big brains, but I got the big——"

"Honestly!" Sandra said, rolling her eyes. "I am sitting right here, you know!"

"I was going to say *heart*," Max joked, putting his hand on his chest.

Sandra snorted and turned up the TV as we walked into the hall.

There wasn't much we could do in Max's room with his mum in the house, so we chatted awkwardly on his bed. After the third long silence, I looked around, searching for another topic of conversation.

"Is that your dad?" I asked, spotting a large photo frame on the wall. Inside was a picture of a man with a mustache, a boy on his knee. "You look cute."

"Have you seen what I'm wearing, though?"

I giggled at the pair of tiny yellow shorts. "How old were you there?"

Max stood up and gazed at the photo. "Dunno. Seven or something."

"Do you miss him?"

"Nah," Max said too loudly.

"He looks nice. Apart from the big mustache."

"That's gone now. Apparently his new girlfriend doesn't like it."

"Can I ask you something?" I said suddenly.

"If you want."

"Was it awful when they split up?" Max flinched so I muttered, "You don't have to answer that. Sorry. It's just that my mum and dad keep arguing, and sometimes I think, you know, that they might actually . . . But anyway. They probably won't." Reaching under his desk with his foot, Max back-heeled a ball and dribbled it around the room without meeting my eyes. "You're good at that."

"Not good enough," he muttered, kicking the ball against the closet.

"Come off it! You're the best in the school, and you know it."

"Yeah, but how many schools are there in the country?" he asked, moving the ball easily between his feet.

"I dunno."

"Have a guess."

"Twenty thousand? Thirty?"

"Say there are twenty-five thousand. That's twenty-five thousand lads, just like me. The best in their school." He kicked the ball to me and surprisingly I managed to pass it back in a straight line. "Twenty-five thousand. And how many people do you think make it as a professional?"

"Absolutely no idea," I muttered, "but I get your point."

"Unlike my brother, who's good at everything, soccer's the only thing I can do, but I can't do it well enough to make a living out of it."

"That sucks."

"Yep." He passed the ball to me, but this time I missed it so it rolled under the bed. I leaned down to grab it but stopped short when I spotted something concealed in the shadows.

"Is that a . . ."

"No!"

"It is!" I exclaimed, pointing at a half-finished jigsaw hidden under his bed. Five hundred pieces, there must have been, spread out on a tray. The completed section showed a soccer stadium with thousands of fans.

"Don't get it out!" he groaned, because I was lifting it onto his duvet.

"This is completely brilliant."

He stared at me uncertainly. "It is?"

"Completely and totally brilliant."

"It's just a jigsaw," he replied, but he seemed pleased.

"Oh no," I said, shaking my head. "This is not just a jigsaw. This is proof."

"Proof of what?"

I batted my eyelashes. "That the Mighty Max Morgan is a secret geek."

"I wouldn't go that far," he said, but we smiled as we arranged the jigsaw between us and got down to work.

It was fun. And hard. There was a lot of field to do, and all the pieces were the exact same color of green. After an hour, we'd finished the section by the corner flag, and we surveyed it, feeling satisfied, before we made our way into the living room. Sandra had fallen asleep on the sofa with her mouth wide open.

"Must've dropped off," she muttered thickly when Max shook her awake.

"Thanks for having me," I said, pulling on my coat. "And for the pizza."

"You're welcome." She smiled sleepily. "How're you getting home?"

"Just going to walk it."

Sandra moved the curtain with her foot. "You can't do that, sweetheart. It's pitch-black out there. Freezing."

"I'll be fine. Honest," I replied, moving toward the door. "I have to set off now, though. Mum wants me back by ten."

Sandra combed her fingers through her hair. "I feel terrible. I'd give you a lift, but I've had too much wine."

"Aaron?" Max suggested.

My stomach twisted guiltily. Nervously. Hopefully. Sandra was already on her feet and hurrying out of the room.

Stuart, you can imagine the tension as I stood outside the house saying good-bye to Max as Aaron climbed into DOR1S.

Even though we'd had a nice time, I tried to escape without being kissed, but Max leaned in close as the car headlights came on. In the glare, he put his hand on my chin and brought his lips to mine. I pictured it from Aaron's point of view, trying to feel good about my revenge, but any sense of glory just bounced around my empty insides, like that phrase *Hollow Victory*.

Max disappeared back into the house. There was just me and Aaron. Aaron and me. Biting the inside of my cheek, I put a foot into his car.

"Sorry about this." Aaron didn't reply. He stared straight ahead and started the engine as I closed the door. "I really appreciate it." He put the car into reverse and moved backward down the drive. "It's freezing out there," I tried again. Aaron turned on the radio.

We drove in silence. Over the crosswalk. Past the church and the Chinese takeout. The emerald dragon whizzed by the window. Aaron gripped the steering wheel, his back poker-straight and his arms thrust out in front, locked at the elbows. Turning down the volume on the radio, I tried once more to strike up conversation.

"How did your studying go?"

Aaron twisted the dial too hard in the opposite direction. The speakers screeched in protest as a singer bellowed *LOVE* just like that, and it sounded big and painful and scary.

We jerked to a stop at a traffic light, Aaron's foot slamming the brake too hard. Miss Scarlet hit the window then swirled in a circle as she hung from the mirror. I tapped her with my finger to make her swing.

"Don't touch that!"

I did it again. Tap. Aaron shook his head and turned off the radio suddenly. *LO—*

"You're such a child," he said. "Everything's a game to you, isn't it?"

I folded my arms. "It's just a stupid Clue figure."

"That's not what I'm talking about," Aaron growled, glaring at the road, his eyes wild. "That's not what I'm talking about, and you know it. What do you think you're playing at? Turning up in my kitchen? Coming to my house?"

"Your brother's house!" I corrected him. "Your *brother's.*"

The traffic light turned green. Aaron put his foot down and the car screeched off.

"So it's like that, is it?"

"You tell me," I replied, gripping onto the dashboard as we sped around a corner. "You're the one who said we were a good couple. You're the one who told me to have fun. So that's what I'm doing. Having fun!"

"Fine!" Aaron yelled.

"It *is* fine," I said, throwing Aaron's words from the party back in his face with spiteful triumph. Hands trembling, throat raw, my finger flew to my chest. "I'm not doing anything wrong, Aaron. I'm free to see whoever I want. You said so yourself."

Tears burned in my eyes. I swiped them away, glowering at Fiction Road.

Fiction Road.

Mum was walking out of the house, about to set off to

Lauren's. Aaron was slowing down, trying to work out which house was mine. Any moment now, Mum would glance this way and see me in the—

"*Drive!*" I screeched, ducking as Mum's eyes fell on Aaron's car. "Please just drive!" Aaron hesitated. Bit his lip. And then hit the accelerator so we roared past my house.

"What's going on?"

"You've got to get to Lauren's! I should've said. That was my mum. She thinks I'm at my friend's house."

Babbling, I told him the directions, choosing a back way that gave us more chance of beating Mum. I was urging the car forward with every ounce of my being, like it was a horse and I was a jockey in the race of my life. We turned right. Screeched left. Powered down a straight road.

Aaron sniffed.

"You should stop telling lies, you know. It's a bad habit."

I looked at him in disbelief. "You really want to continue this now?"

"I'm just saying. You should stop lying. It's—"

"It's what?"

He paused. Took a breath. Pronounced the word clearly. "*Immature.*"

I forced out a laugh. "Immature? Who's got Miss Scarlet hanging off their mirror? Who talks about ghosts and alligators and black holes full of snakes? Who hasn't got a plan and doesn't know what they're going to do in the future and—"

"Don't change the subject," Aaron snapped. "You lied to your mum and it was wrong and that's the end of it."

"Who says it's the end of it? You? Just because you're older? Give me a break, Aaron. You have no right to tell me what I can and can't do. What I tell my mum has nothing to do with you. *Nothing.*"

Aaron lifted a shoulder. "Maybe not. But what you tell *me* is pretty important, and you lied to my face."

A traffic light turned red as we approached it. I swore under my breath, glancing at the time on my phone. 9:55 PM.

"You told me your grandpa was dead."

Red

Red

Red

Green

"*Go!*" I shouted, and we sped off again. 9:56 PM.

"But you weren't visiting his grave that day I saw you," Aaron pressed.

"No, but . . ."

"You'd been in my house. *My* house!" He was shouting now and his words rang in my ears. "With *my* brother!"

"I know, but . . ."

"In *his* bedroom. And you had the cheek, the nerve, to get into my car and pretend that you'd—"

"Enough!" I roared, slamming my fist onto my thigh. "*Enough.*"

9:59 PM.

Aaron pulled onto Lauren's street. I leaned up on my seat, scanning the road for Mum's car with frantic eyes. The coast was clear. Pulling open the door, I made to get out.

181

"You're welcome," Aaron said sarcastically.

"Oh, grow up," I spat, climbing out of the car, the air freezing against my hot cheeks. "Thanks *so* much for the lift. It's been great."

"I don't know how you could do it, Zoe!" Aaron called, his eyes blazing in the darkness. "I don't know how you could've acted like such a bitch!"

"You never gave me a chance to explain!"

I slammed the door as the clock hit 10 PM. Aaron revved the engine and tore down the road, and I swore at him loudly, all the worst words I could think of. The wind swirled and my body trembled and my blood boiled underneath my flushed skin.

"Good night?" Mum asked a couple of minutes later as I collapsed onto the seat, hiding my anger. The fib caught in my throat, but I thought of Aaron and forced it out defiantly.

"Not bad. You know. For a Geography project."

I think I'm going to leave it here tonight. I really want to tell you what happened next, but I can barely keep my eyes open. The last few nights have been interrupted with bad dreams. I keep jolting awake, cold and clammy as the rain pours and the smoke swirls and the hand disappears over and over again. I'm not quite ready to talk about it yet, but I will. One day soon. That's a promise. We've still got a bit of time before May 1 if the worst happens and the nun can't put a stop to it. There must be something we can do so don't give up yet, thinking you deserve this punishment for your mistakes. As you can see, I made them, too. You're not on your own, Stu, so don't lie there on your thin mattress believing that the whole world just sees your bad soul. There's a girl in England who knows there's some good.

Love,

Zoe xx

1 Fiction Road

Bath, UK

S. Harris #993765
Polunsky Unit (Death Row)
Livingston, Texas 77351
USA
February 13

Hey there, Stu,

The spider's not been around for a few weeks, but there are a couple of new webs by the door so I reckon she's lurking in the shadows, watching me scribble and copying my words, spelling out my secrets on the ceiling in silver silk. Or maybe that's the paranoia kicking in, which FYI is hardly surprising given what happened today after school.

I stayed behind to talk to my old Religious Education teacher, and you'll be pleased to know why because I was asking about the nun.

"Why do you want to write to her?" Mr. Andrews said, scribbling something about Jesus on the whiteboard in purple marker, ready for his class the following morning.

"Because," I began, trying to pluck up the courage to tell the lie I'd planned.

"*Because*," Mr. Andrews mocked, drawing a stickman on a crucifix.

"I found God."

"Where?" He drew a speech bubble from Jesus's mouth and scrawled *AAARRRGH* in block capitals. *AAARRRGH* indeed. I hadn't expected that question.

"In my . . . pencil case, sir."

"Borrowing an eraser, was he?"

"No. When I opened my pencil case in math, light reflected off the lid and made a cross on the table."

"Moving," Mr. Andrews said. "Truly." He threw the board marker onto his desk. "She's from a convent in Edinburgh. St. Catherine's. And her name is Janet."

Janet will be receiving a letter soon, Stu. Don't you worry about that. As I walked out of school enjoying the sun on my face, I felt positive for the first time in months. I rushed all the way home to start my campaign, planning to print off your poems to send to the nun and to write all your good qualities in a bullet-point list to make it clear you're:

- a good listener
- understanding
- creative
- similar to Harry Potter because—

And that's when I saw it.
DOR1S.

Parked outside my house.

A pair of brown eyes followed my progress along the pavement.

"Hi," I called from the other side of the road.

"Where've you been? I've been waiting for you."

"My Religious Education teacher. I stayed behind to talk to him. Why are you driving...I mean, why are you in his car?"

"Mine's having a service," Sandra explained. "This one's been sitting in the garage for months."

I couldn't take my eyes off it. The old blue doors. The dented roof.

"Is everything okay?" I asked as Sandra beckoned me over. I caught sight of my reflection in the car window. Pale cheeks. Wary eyes. Thinner than I'd realized.

Sandra smiled suddenly, but it looked odd. Too intense. "I've got some good news." She undid her seat belt, and I recoiled slightly as she stepped out of the car. "There's going to be a memorial service."

"A what?"

"I only thought of it this afternoon, and I came straight here to tell you. I want to mark the first anniversary. Do something special for him." She put her bony hand on my shoulder, completely misreading my horrified expression. "Don't worry. You'll be involved, too. A reading or something."

"No!" I said, and Sandra blinked, though her smile didn't fade. "I don't know if I can do that. Not in front of everyone."

She increased the pressure on my shoulder. "I know it's hard, but we need to do something to keep his memory alive," and Stu I almost laughed out loud. As if it would ever fade. As if it was that easy. She leaned back into the car and pulled a notepad out of her handbag. "I've got some ideas," she said, flicking through pages and pages of her messy handwriting. "Have you got time to hear one or two?"

"Flute lesson," I blurted out, making it up on the spot.

"Oh. Okay. Never mind, then." She closed the notepad. "Maybe some other time."

"Sure," I said, walking away as fast as I could. "See you later."

Before I reached my drive, she called, "When, exactly?"

I stalled. "Whenever you like," I said, without turning around.

"Shall I ring you? You can come over. Maybe this weekend. We can plan it together."

I closed my eyes, trying to hide my growing anger. "I'm busy this weekend."

"All weekend?"

"Well, no, but—"

"I'll call you, then," she said, and I turned around to see her climb back into the car, hitting Miss Scarlet with her shoulder. The red figure swung from side to side, and I missed Aaron with a pain that gnawed on every bone in my body, like toothache all over. A year ago I felt exactly the same, pining for him after the argument, when he didn't call and he didn't call and he didn't call.

*   *   *

With Aaron out of the equation, there was no real need to stop things with his brother. Besides, things had improved since the night of the jigsaw so we became a fixed pair that kind of went together even though it was a bit odd, like peanut butter and jelly, which I'm guessing might be one of your favorites. Of course I stayed clear of his house, but whenever I could think of an excuse to tell Mum, we hung out in town, nearly always by the river because it was quiet and there was a bench with trees hanging over it to protect us if it rained.

Grandpa was moved from the hospital to a care home, and Dad was helping him get settled in, visiting as much as possible. On Valentine's Day, he came downstairs with a card, dropping it on top of the pile of ironing Mum was doing in the kitchen as I ate my breakfast before school. Mum didn't acknowledge it, just watched Dad chuck a bag onto the floor and some bread into the toaster, the iron steaming on Dot's trousers.

"You off there again?"

"Taking him some more photos," Dad replied. "It's working. Honestly. His speech is getting better, too. Last time he said the Lord's Prayer with hardly any mistakes. The nurses have been brilliant. Really impressive. We're working together to try to get him—"

"Shame they're not paying you."

"I'm looking for a job, too," Dad replied, peering into the toaster.

"Well, you won't find one in there." She folded the jeans

then took the Valentine's card off the pile of clothes and tore it open. For a second, her face softened. "Thank you, Simon." Dad looked pleased with himself as he buttered his toast.

Now Stu I'm sure you must celebrate Valentine's Day in America, probably much bigger than we do over here, because I've seen on TV how your country goes mad for holidays. I reckon you used to do loads for Alice before she told you about the affair with your brother, e.g., candles and petals leading to a candlelit meal on your balcony, or maybe you left a trail of ketchup packets instead so your wife could follow them to the cheeseburger and curly fries and milk shake with two straws.

I didn't love Max, but what choice did I have but to send him a card, so I bought him one with a polar bear in a bikini and gave it to him at lunchtime. The words inside said *You make me hot*, and I added . . . *Like global warming*. Max stared at it blankly, but I knew Aaron would have laughed. My stomach twisted as I sat down with my tray. I told myself off with this harsh voice in my head, chewing my chicken nuggets with more determination than usual, eager to giggle at Max's jokes, but he didn't tell a single one, just picked miserably at a few chips.

After school we had an hour together because Mum was taking Dot to speech therapy so we made our way down to the river. Chaffinches flew from branch to branch as we found our usual bench. Max picked up a stone and started to scratch something on the wood as a heron swooped out of the sky to land near my feet.

"Look!" I exclaimed, pointing at the huge bird dipping its yellow beak into the water. Max barely glanced at it. "Are you okay?" I asked, fed up with his mood. "You've been grumpy all day."

"I'm good."

"You don't look it."

The stone stopped moving. "It's Tuesday."

"So?"

"I see my dad on Tuesdays. Normally, anyway. But whatever." Max started on the bench again. "He's taking his girlfriend out for a meal. I don't care, though," he said quickly. "Doesn't bother me."

"Of course it does," I replied gently. "And that's okay." He nodded so imperceptibly I might have imagined it, then stood up quickly. The heron took off from the water with a huge flap of wings. Dropping the stone, Max pointed at the bench.

MM + ZJ
Feb 14

"Happy Valentine's Day, girlfriend," he muttered. "You know. If you want to be."

He looked so awkward and nervous that I reached out for his hand and just said, "Yes."

Even as the word left my lips, I knew it felt wrong, and Soph detected it, too, lying on her bed with her head dangling off the edge, looking at me upside down, her cheeks turning purple as they filled with blood.

"So you're not an *Or What* anymore?" she said when I got home.

"No."

"You don't sound very pleased about it."

"I am," I lied. "'Course I am. It's Max, isn't it? Everyone wants to be with him."

"You gonna tell Mum?"

I lay down next to her and tipped back my own head, my hair touching the carpet. "I don't have a death wish."

"She probably wouldn't care anyway," Soph said. "Too busy worrying about Dot."

"More like Dad," I said, because he still wasn't back from visiting Grandpa and Mum was seething. A temp agency had left a message on his cell saying there were a couple of weeks' work, but Dad had missed it because he'd forgotten to take his phone. Downstairs I could hear Mum pacing pacing pacing, stopping every now and again, no doubt to open the curtains and check the drive. "I wish he'd get a job. Or that Grandpa would get better."

"Or die."

"Soph!"

"I'm only joking!" she said, sliding off the bed and onto the rug, holding her head and blinking ten times as the blood went back to normal. "But it would be nice to get some money in his will."

"What would you do with it? Say, if you got thousands of pounds?"

She lolled onto her back, spread-eagled on the floor. "Move somewhere sunny with a pool and a new house and a big hutch for hundreds of rabbits and a new school just around the corner."

"How is it?" I asked, feeling guilty. I'd been so wrapped up with Aaron and Max, I hadn't checked for a while. "Any better?" Soph hesitated, fiddling with the mood ring on her finger. "Are they still doing it?"

"Sort of."

"What do you mean, sort of?"

"It was okay for a while, but now the names are really bad."

I struggled to twist around on the bed. "Like what?"

"Don't want to say." She picked fluff off the carpet, not meeting my eyes. "But last week Portia hit me."

"She *hit* you? Where?"

"Not hard," Soph said quickly. "Not enough to make a bruise or anything, but it still hurt."

"We have to tell Mum. We really do, Soph."

Slowly, she nodded. I stayed with her for ages, turning on her TV when she climbed into bed so she wouldn't hear the inevitable argument when Dad got home, not that my plan worked, because there was such an almighty row that Stu you probably heard it in Texas.

"I forgot, all right? It was a mistake!" Dad roared.

"You probably left your phone here on purpose so you wouldn't have to—"

"I *want* a job! Why do you think I've been filling out hundreds of applications?"

"Don't exaggerate!" Mum bickered as I listened on the stairs. "Hundreds? Please!"

"Well, I've done a *hundred* percent more than you."

"I keep this place running!" Mum argued. "If it wasn't for me—"

"If it wasn't for you, we'd all breathe a little easier! You're too controlling, Jane. And I tell you something, I'm putting my foot down. I've had enough."

I imagined Mum and Dad eyeballing each other from opposite sides of the room.

"Is this about your father?"

"Partly," Dad admitted, and there was no apology in his voice. "You can't stop my children from seeing my dad, Jane. It isn't fair."

"It isn't suitable for them to see him!" Mum groaned. "This is precisely why I don't trust your judgment, Simon. Expecting me to let our kids go into a care home to talk to a mental—"

"Don't speak about my dad like that," Dad warned, and in my head, I watched him hold out a shaking finger. "Don't you dare."

"I *do* dare!" Mum yelled. "I can have an opinion. It's our money you're spending, driving miles every day to see that man when you should be doing something more useful."

"Money I've earned!"

"Money you're *no longer* earning," Mum corrected him. "Money we can't afford to spend, because you can't get a damn job!"

"I won't take employment advice from someone who refuses to work."

"My job's here," Mum started. "With the girls. Someone has to look out for them and stop you from doing something dangerous."

"Taking my children to visit their grandpa is not dangerous!"

"It's ridiculous!"

"*You're* ridiculous! It wouldn't do them any harm at all. You're not letting them grow up. Or be independent. Or exposed to the world."

"I'm the one who wants Dot to have the implant so she can hear the bloody world!"

"She's happy!" Dad argued. "Really happy!"

"She's struggling, Simon. That's what the speech therapist told me today. She's not picking up the lip-reading as quickly as she might and—"

"She can sign, and she's doing well at school with the help of her assistants. There's no need to send her to the hospital again, to disrupt her like that."

"She'll be able to hear, though," Mum said in a wobbly voice. "Music. The TV. Me."

"She'll be able to hear a whole load of electronic buzzing and squeaking that's nothing like the real world. And it might not even work. You saw what happened last time! No," Dad said firmly. "It's not worth the risk. You're being selfish!"

"Selfish? I'm doing this for our daughter!"

"You're doing it for yourself," Dad spat, "and we both know it!"

"What's that supposed to mean?"

"You know what I'm talking about! You want Dot to be able to hear because it's your fault that she's—"

"*GET OUT!*" Mum bellowed suddenly, and the words echoed through the whole house. "*GO!*"

I didn't for a second think that he'd leave, but the living room door slammed. The front one, too. I clung on to the banister, breathing shakily. I stared at my toes, not sure what to do, and then hinges creaked as Soph's eyes appeared in the gap of her door, huge and terrified. I told her to go back to sleep, but Mum started crying in the living room so we both ran downstairs.

"Mum?" My voice sounded quiet after the argument. "Mum, are you okay?"

She was hunched on the leather sofa, her back quivering. "I'm . . . I'm fine."

Soph charged over and forced herself onto Mum's lap, putting her arms around her neck.

"You don't look fine. What was all that about?" I asked, sounding frustrated and not bothering to cover it up. Grandpa and Mum and her job and Dot—none of it made sense. "What was your fault? What did Dad mean?"

"Nothing." Mum wiped her eyes, her voice quivering.

"It's not nothing!" I exploded. I stood in front of Mum with my expression probably furious. "Dad just walked out!"

"He'll be back in five minutes when he's calmed down," Mum replied, heaving Soph off her lap. "You're a bit heavy, my love." She stood up and took a deep breath then wiped her nose on her sleeve. "He can be so bloody stubborn. Not wanting Dot to have something that could help her. Pressuring me to take you to see Grandpa when he knows full well what happened."

"What *did* happen?"

"Well, I won't be bullied," Mum said, tucking her hair behind her ears, not listening to a word I was saying. "Absolutely not."

"Soph's being bullied," I said in this pointed sort of way. "*Actually* bullied. By girls in her class." Mum spun around to look at her, and Soph fiddled with the sleeve of her pajama top. "It's been going on awhile, and it's getting worse. You need to do something because it's getting really bad. Not just names and stuff. This girl called Portia *hit* her."

"What?"

"It's true," I said, seeing the shocked expression on Mum's face and hoping that she was coming to her senses. "I just thought you should know there are things going on apart from you and Dad."

That's when he walked back into the house with a newspaper tucked underneath his arm, his light eye gray and stormy. Neither of them apologized. Mum watched Dad sit on the armchair, and Dad watched Mum straighten the clothes on the radiator. I have no idea what they were thinking, but Stu I'm pretty certain it was nothing about gold silk or rock pools or starlight.

Love,
Zoe xx
1 Fiction Road
Bath, UK

S. Harris #993765
Polunsky Unit (Death Row)
Livingston, Texas 77351
USA
March 3

Hey there, Stu,

Less than two months to go. I wonder if you've marked your calendar with a cross on May 1, or maybe you've just written 6 *PM lethal injection*, and all I can say is I hope you're not afraid of needles like Lauren, who fainted twice at school vaccinations and almost swallowed her tongue. It must be so strange to know when you're going to die. All that buildup of tension. Sort of like Christmas, but without the turkey, unless you've ordered that for your final meal. Anyway, it might not come to that so let's not start fantasizing about all the trimmings, because who knows, you might have another few years if the nun's got anything to do with it. No one knows what's going to happen a month from now or two months from now, and that's what I keep telling myself when I get nervous about the memorial.

It's taking place at school because Sandra got the go-ahead from the staff to hire the hall for a two-course dinner on May 1, prepared by the lunch ladies.

"It's going to be nice," she said in the sunroom last weekend as Mum smiled and I thought about honoring someone with spotted dick and custard. "And it'll raise money for the school as well. Fifteen pounds per ticket. You'll get yours free, of course," she added, patting my leg. I moved it out of the way, pretending to have an itch on my knee. "Have you thought any more about what you might like to read?"

I didn't reply. I couldn't. The sun burst through the clouds, fastening me to the sofa like a hot gold thumbtack.

"You've been quite busy at school, haven't you?" Mum said as sweat crept out of my pores.

"Well, I think it would be nice to have something personal. Something she's written herself," Sandra went on as if I wasn't there. "Something from her heart."

"You'll be good at that, Zo," Mum replied, taking my hand and rubbing my palm with her thumb. "You're a lovely writer." It was the first time she'd ever said anything like that. "I know you'll come up with something perfect."

It was a nice thing to say, but Stu when I tried to do it earlier, all I managed was his name underlined five times. Scrunching up the paper, I threw it in the trash with a roar of frustration and stamped on it hard, which hurt my foot, but I deserved it so I did it again and again, hating myself for the pain that I've caused and the things that I've done. It would be bliss to forget, to be like Grandpa after the stroke, confused and dazed, tossing memories to the side and asking for a bowl of strawberry jelly.

If I can't forget, then I need to get it out, now more than ever, because Stu we don't have long. No matter how hard it is, I have to keep going because you're the only one who understands. If everything goes wrong on May 1, my chance will be gone. You'll die not knowing the worst of me when I know the worst of you, and that's not fair. We're in this together, so don't worry, I'll keep talking till the very end to keep you distracted and stop you from feeling alone in your cell, which I'm guessing seems smaller than ever, the outside world even farther away.

We'll start with Dot's sixth birthday on February 18 so imagine her waking me up by leaping onto my bed, actually my head, if I remember rightly, banging it with her knee.

"It's my special day!" She signed the words in front of my face so I could see her hands. Her little finger skimmed my nose.

"I know it is."

"So where's my present?"

I pretended to gasp. "I forgot!"

Dot screwed up her eyes. "You're lying."

"No. Really. I forgot." Dot grabbed my ears and examined my expression closely, her nose touching mine.

"Liar!" She danced around, signing wildly. "Liar liar liar!"

Laughing, I climbed out of bed and opened my cupboard, reaching for the present hidden underneath my shoes. Dot tore off the wrapping paper to find a gold plastic crown with the words QUEEN OF THE WORLD on the front. She gazed at it in wonder.

"Do you like it?"

"I love it!"

We sat on my bedroom carpet and sipped imaginary tea in Buckingham Palace.

"Can I tell you a secret?" she signed. I ate a pretend biscuit and waited. "You're the best one in the family. The *real* best."

I touched her cheek with my imaginary teacup. "Thanks."

"This is the best present I ever got. Better than what Mum bought me." Dot wrinkled her nose. "Books. And *coloring*. She didn't get me what I asked for."

"What was that?"

Dot stared back at me, her face sad. "New ears."

"Is that why you asked for an iPod from Santa?" I asked, pulling her onto my lap. "Did you ask him, too? For new ears?"

She nodded. "But only in the PS at the bottom of my letter, so maybe he didn't see it."

"Maybe," I managed, aching for her, rocking her from side to side.

She gazed up at me, her eyes really green. "Why was I born like this?"

"I don't know. You can't choose these things."

"Well, I don't think it's fair."

"No," I replied. "Me, neither."

I couldn't stop thinking about her all morning. In the shower. Having breakfast. On the way to the library. Honest truth, I barely listened to Mrs. Simpson bang on about the decorating she was doing at home as I fixed some old books at the main desk.

". . . so in the end I just went for an olive-green carpet."

"Great." I picked at a roll of tape with my thumb, wondering if this was how worried Mum felt about Dot every single day.

"I mean, I briefly considered the *sage* green, but I thought it was a little intense."

"Really."

"Honestly, Zoe, I've never seen sage that color in my life, and I should know because I do a lot of cooking, which is precisely what I said to the salesman. No, I think I've made the correct choice. Olive green is better. Calmer."

"Yeah, definitely."

"And cheaper, incidentally, so I could—isn't that your friend?" Mrs. Simpson asked.

"Absolutely," I said, not listening.

"Over there? By the spiral staircase?"

She pointed a book at a figure and I gasped. Aaron was moving along the Literature shelves, searching for a book, paying no attention to me whatsoever. He scratched his head, looking baffled, no doubt on purpose, wanting me to go up and offer to help. I screwed up a label. Stood up. Lost my nerve. Sat back down again. My leg jiggled under the desk, and then I jumped to my feet. Tipping the Returns box upside down, I prayed there was something from the Literature section.

Two books on knitting patterns.

One on bridges.

An encyclopedia about religion that I tossed aside and swore.

I stuck my hand into the box and there, in the corner, was something else. I pulled it out quickly. A novel by George Eliot! Hugging the book to my chest, I moved toward the stairs. Aaron had grabbed a book, too, and was reading the blurb, walking away from the shelf, and Stu if he had any idea that I was hurrying toward him, it didn't show in his face. I started going up the stairs as he started coming down, twisting and turning, our feet making the metal sing. We met in the exact middle of the spiral, and it was like standing in a great swirl of Aaron's DNA, and I was surrounded by him and wrapped up in him as the rest of the world faded to nothing.

"Fancy seeing you here," I said. I even smiled, utterly convinced he'd come to make amends.

"It's a library, isn't it? I needed a book." His tone surprised me. Winded me, actually. Aaron held up something by Dickens. "For my essay, due on Monday. I left my copy at college. That's the only reason I'm here."

I held up my own book and pointed at the first floor. "Yeah, well. This is the only reason I'm here. I have to return this book to the shelf."

We glowered at each other, but there was something bigger than anger in our eyes. Neither of us moved. Neither of us *wanted* to move. I was blocking his way and he was blocking mine, and we just kept standing there and standing there, people moving above our heads and below our feet as we hung suspended between two floors.

The air was alive. Full. Buzzing and humming and crackling like that static before a storm.

"You shouldn't have called me a bitch," I said at last.

"You shouldn't have acted like one," he replied, but still we stared into each other's eyes, remembering that night and all the others before. The owl. The bonfire. The wall near my house. The window with our trembling hands. A thousand missed opportunities.

"Can you move, please?" Aaron forced out. A thousand and one.

Too disappointed to refuse, I stepped to the side to let him through. Our bodies brushed past each other, and he felt it, too, I was sure of it, a searing burn on the skin as the staircase rattled in a way that shook our bones.

As I made my way up to the first floor, a fat man approached, asking about the Crime section.

"Are there any books by American writers? Other than Grisham, I mean." Down below, Aaron was handing over his card at the librarian's desk. There was a flash of brown—his eyes flicking in my direction—and a flush of pink when he realized that I'd noticed. "I've read every book he's written. Except *The Pelican Brief*, but I saw the film so I know the plot." My lips ached with all the things I wanted to say. Needed to say. "Of course, it's not quite the same as reading it, but—"

"I'm sorry," I interrupted as Mrs. Simpson scanned Aaron's book and stamped the date and he set off toward the exit. "Sorry. I just have to . . ." The sentence trailed off as I charged down the stairs. "*Wait*," I urged under my breath, racing past the desk as Mrs. Simpson hissed my name. My hands slammed against the cold glass door, and I left it spinning as I darted across the foyer and out into the rain—proper English rain, falling in lines, not dots, splattering my skin and soaking my hair and drenching my clothes. Frantic, I looked around, straining my eyes and my neck as I searched the busy pavement for Aaron, but it was hopeless. He had gone.

Back in the foyer, I sank to the floor by the radiator, sitting on my heels, my head in my hands. That was it. My one chance, over—but then I heard a toilet flush, and sure enough, Aaron appeared from the bathroom, wiping his hands on his jeans. Scrambling to my feet, I dashed over, my shoes squelching and my bangs smeared against my forehead. Maybe it was wishful thinking, but Aaron's lips seemed to twitch as I dripped all over the floor, and Stu I didn't mean that to be a metaphor, but perhaps it was, because everything inside me melted at the hint of his grin.

"Look, Aaron, I didn't know, okay?" I blurted out. "I didn't know you were brothers. Not at first." If there had been a smile, it vanished instantly. "I kissed Max the first time because you disappeared. That's the only reason! You have to believe me."

"I didn't disappear for long," Aaron muttered, crossing his arms. "I only went down the road to answer my phone because my mum called and she didn't know we were having a party."

"I searched for you," I said, my hands held out. "I searched everywhere! And at the bonfire I only kissed Max because I was upset you had a girlfriend."

"But I don't have a g—"

"I know that now!" I said, wiping rain off my face in frustration. "But I really thought you were together. I swear to God."

Aaron rolled his eyes. "So, what, you just jumped to conclusions and went off with my brother?"

"I didn't *know* you were brothers when all this started," I cried, desperate for him to believe me. "How could I have known? I would never have—"

"But you found out!" Aaron replied. "You found out we were brothers, and you carried on."

"Only because you told me to!"

"So you're just using him?" Aaron asked.

"No, I mean . . . Look, it's not as if I don't *like* Max, because I do. I really like him, but—" With a snarl of rage, Aaron put up his hood and stormed out of the door. I charged after him, seizing his arm and spinning him around before he had chance to disappear down the road. "We're not leaving it like this!" I yelled as rain splashed against my skin.

"Like what?" Aaron shouted, yanking his arm away. His chest was rising and falling and our pulses were racing and I had to make him understand.

"With you thinking that I chose Max!"

"You did choose him!"

"Because I didn't know that *you* were an option!"

And without thinking about it, without worrying about the consequences, I grabbed Aaron's face and pulled it toward mine, our mouths meeting with such force that it hurt in the sweetest way.

We broke apart, shock on our faces. For a few seconds,

nothing happened. Nothing happened and everything happened, because in that instant we didn't express a single word of regret and we both smiled with a happiness that was bigger than any guilt. Looking all around to make sure no one could see, Aaron clutched my hand and we started to run, adrenaline humming in our veins as we charged, desperate to find somewhere to be alone. The rain doubled in force like nature was on our side, trapping people indoors. The buildings and the cobbles and the steps and the alleyways and the churches and the parks—everything, the entire city, belonged to us for one precious moment that was long and wide, and Stu we filled every last bit of it.

This was living.

Really living.

Colors were brighter. Smells stronger. Sounds louder. I heard every glug of water bursting out of a drain, saw every bare branch as we sprinted past trees, smelled every bit of rain and mud and fumes as we took shelter in a tower that led up to the city wall. Aaron kissed me in the musty darkness, his lips soft but his fingers urgent. I could smell him, Stu—toothpaste and soap and deodorant, nothing special—but I closed my eyes and breathed him in as our mouths moved and our bodies pressed and our feet got wet in a puddle we barely noticed.

Love,

Zoe xx

1 Fiction Road

Bath, UK

S. Harris #993765
Polunsky Unit (Death Row)
Livingston, Texas 77351
USA
March 17

Hey there, Stu,

It's a relief to be in here with you tonight. There's a blanket that
Dot must have left so I've curled up under that on the deck chair,
happy to be hidden away. Honest truth, I don't know how long I
can keep up the pretense anymore, like imagine an actress in *The
Wizard of Oz* messing up her lines, the witch's green makeup dripping onto the stage. Except for me, of course, it's the opposite, my
good face melting away to reveal something bad underneath. The
audience screams. Mum. Dad. Sandra the loudest of all.

She turned up again this evening. Unannounced. Ringing
the doorbell three times and stepping into the hall without waiting for an invitation.

"What's she doing here?" Dot signed. "And why hasn't she washed her hair?"

"Dot says hello," Dad muttered, showing Sandra into the living room, being all "How are things" and "Nice to see you," though I could tell he was shocked by her sudden appearance.

"She smells funny," Dot signed.

"My daughter's got a cold," Dad explained because Dot was waving her hand in front of her nose. "What can I do for you, Sandra?"

He pointed at an armchair, but Sandra knelt on the floor, where I was sitting. Her T-shirt wasn't much protection against the cold night, and her thin arms were covered in purplish goose bumps. Dot wasn't exaggerating about the smell. As Sandra turned her bag upside down and shook, I caught a strong whiff of alcohol on her breath. Photos fell onto the carpet by my feet.

"For the display. At the memorial. I thought you might like to see them."

Before I could respond, Dad frowned and said, "Did you drive here, Sandra?"

Sandra just grinned, her lips stained with wine. "Look at this one," she said, holding up a photo of a little boy on his front with talcum powder all over his chubby legs. "And this!"

"Fat baby." Dot again.

"Cute," Dad said. "Very cute."

Slippers shuffled on the carpet as Mum walked in with a book in her hand, stopping dead when she spotted Sandra spreading photos over the rug.

"What's going on?"

"That lady's gone crazy," Dot signed.

"Sandra's come to show us some pictures," Dad said, glaring at Dot, who giggled. "Isn't that nice?"

A toddler with a chocolate-covered smile.

A nine-year-old with a scab on his knee.

First school photo.

Last school photo.

A photo of me at the Spring Fair standing between two brothers.

Sandra passed it to me, and I took it with hands that wouldn't stop shaking. Someone would see them, I was sure of it, so I dropped the picture onto my lap and pressed my fingers between my knees, hating the clamminess of my skin. My face—that was impossible, too. I tried a smile, but my lips felt wrong.

"You wouldn't guess that something terrible was about to happen," Sandra said softly, peering at the photo. "There's been something I've been meaning to ask you, actually. Something about that night."

"I'm not sure Zoe's up to it," Mum said quickly, seeing my face drain of color. "She doesn't like to talk about the Spring Fair."

"But it's important."

"I think it's better if we just look at these photos," Mum said. "I'm sure there are some lovely ones."

"Why did you leave?" Sandra persisted, and though she might have had a drink, her gaze was steady.

"I told you before. We went for a walk," I said too quickly.

"But why?"

"That's a nice one," Mum said, pointing at a picture of Max and Aaron and Fiona on three mountain bikes. "Very sweet. Let's have a look at some others." She made to pick up a photo, but Sandra gathered them into a pile.

"If you don't mind, I want to understand my son's last movements."

My heart was frantic, slamming against my ribs, trying to get away from the questions as I jumped to my feet. "It's hard for me," I said. My eyes filled with tears. "It's hard for me to discuss it. Impossible. I dream about that night all the time, and I'm scared of thinking about it because it still feels so—"

"Easy, love," Mum said as Dad put his hand on my sweaty back.

Sandra blushed, clutching the photos tightly. "I'm sorry. I just—I don't understand why you left the fair. Through the woods. Where were you going?"

"Nowhere. We got bored," I lied. "That's all. We got bored."

"If only you hadn't," Sandra muttered, and Stu that's when I walked out of the room on shaky legs, pretending I wanted to make a cup of tea. Ten minutes later, I was still staring at the kettle. It was Mum who had to flick the switch.

Love,
Zoe xxx
1 Fiction Road
Bath, UK

S. Harris #993765
Polunsky Unit (Death Row)
Livingston, Texas 77351
USA
April 1

My dear Stu,

In the end, I told Sandra I couldn't do the speech at the memorial service. I ran around to her house and battered down the door and sprinted into the sunroom, roaring the word "*No!*"

Sandra looked up from the photos with narrowed eyes. "What?"

"No. Just no!" I shouted, and I even pointed my trembling finger in her face. "*No.*"

April Fools', Stu.

Sometimes at night, I pretend that the past few months have been a big joke. Lying in the darkness, I tell myself that this is not my life. All I have to do is wait until 12 PM and Sandra will turn around and shout "Got you!" and a voice in the coffin will say "April Fools'!" and I will laugh and laugh and laugh until tears fall down my face. The prison guards will open up your cell and you will dance out of Death Row with the lightest heart you've ever had in your chest and your wife will be waiting for you at home with no stab wounds to speak of.

Let's pretend for just one moment that could actually happen. You close your eyes and I'll close mine, and let's dream the same dream across the Atlantic, lighting up the darkness between us. Can you see it, Stu? Can you see us up there, shining in all the black?

Me, neither.

I hate to say it, but I don't think the nun's going to come to your rescue, even though the letter that I sent was six sides of A4. I mean, perhaps I'm wrong, but I haven't seen anything about a protest on Google. Maybe I never really believed it would happen, because I don't feel that shocked that she's not standing outside the prison with a petition. Maybe I never expected us to have a happy ending. At least we've got each other, Stu, for the next few days. That means a lot to me and I hope it means a lot to you, and I suppose I should get on, so let's start where we left off, with wet toes in soggy shoes squelching back to the library.

We had it all worked out by the time we said good-bye in the foyer. Aaron was going to explain everything to Max that week-end before I saw him in school, where I would talk to him, too. Then me and Aaron were going to take it slow and not rub his nose in it, waiting for Max to move on before I came around to the house. By the end of my shift, I'd convinced myself that Max would get over it in probably less than two weeks, choosing one of the thousands of other girls at school who were interested.

"You look happy," Mum said when I climbed into the car.

My whole face seemed to twinkle as I grinned. "My shift was very rewarding."

"Come off it! A look like that can only mean one thing."

"*Mum!*"

"I remember what it was like to be young, you know. Vaguely, anyway. Who is he, then?"

"No one!" I cried, the tips of my ears pink.

"*No one* must be very nice indeed," she said, checking her mirrors before setting off. "Be careful, though, won't you? I don't really like the idea of you getting distracted by boys."

"I'm not getting distracted by anyone."

"Good. Because boys come and go, you know. Not like exam grades. They'll stay with you forever."

"Romantic," I muttered as we pulled out onto the road. The rain had stopped, but the tires splashed through puddles, and I loved the noise it made, and the gray sky lurking above the trees, and the traffic, and the shops, and the whole ordinary extraordinary world.

"It's the truth, my love. There'll be time for boys in the future, but you've got one chance at school and—" She stopped herself when I sighed. "Sorry."

I glanced at her, surprised. "It's okay."

"No, it isn't." She blew out her cheeks. "Maybe . . . oh, I don't know . . . Maybe your dad had a point about me." She tapped my knee. "Don't tell him I said that, though."

We drove the rest of the way in silence, both of us lost in thought. As we parked outside the house, Soph peeped out of her bedroom window but completely ignored my wave, swiping her curtains closed.

"What's up with her?" I asked, stepping out onto the driveway.

"I'm afraid she isn't in the best of moods," Mum said. "Those girls at school . . ."

"Are they getting worse?"

Mum shook her head. "Not exactly." She opened the trunk and handed me a birthday cake for Dot in a big white box. "Don't drop that! It was expensive." She picked up three more bags and followed me into the house, telling me to take off my shoes at the door. "I spoke to Soph's teacher yesterday."

"Did you tell her about Portia?"

"I did."

"And what did she say?"

Mum lowered her voice. "That there isn't a Portia in Soph's class."

"Well, she must be in a different—"

"And there isn't one in the whole school," Mum finished as the white box almost ended up on the carpet. "She made it up, Zo. All of it."

Before I could take this in, Dot charged out of the living room in her new crown, signing excitedly.

"Is that my princess cake?"

"Just as you ordered!" Mum replied. "How's my special birthday girl?"

"Let me see! Let me see!"

Mum put down the bags and lifted the lid of the white box. Dot's eyes shone as she gazed at the pink icing then she shot upstairs, bursting into Soph's room.

"Get out!" Soph roared.

"Goodness, she can be so moody," Mum muttered. "Not a wonder, really, with all the lies she's been telling. Confronted her this morning. She admitted that she'd made it all up. Wouldn't tell me why she'd done it, though."

I made my way into the kitchen and put the box on the table, talking over my shoulder. "Well, that bit is obvious. She's jealous, isn't she?"

"Of what?" Mum asked, grabbing six candles, stopping to admire the cake.

"Dot."

Mum looked up quickly. "Why would she be jealous of her?"

I shrugged. "You spend all your time with her."

Mum held out a candle to push into the cake then paused with her arm outstretched. "I have to, Zoe. She can't *hear*. . . ."

"You don't need to explain to me. I get it," I said, and for the first time, I thought I actually did. "It's hard to see Dot struggle."

Mum swallowed, clutching the candles tighter. "Exactly."

"But Soph's struggling too, Mum. If you're not dealing with Dot, you're arguing with Dad about Grandpa or jobs or money, and it's hard listening to you fight all the time. I'm sorry," I said quickly, thinking I'd said far too much.

Mum sat down suddenly, staring at the candles in her hand. I made to leave, but before I could walk out of the kitchen, she said, "Tell Soph I want to talk to her, will you?"

I have no idea what was said, but Soph's eyes were red and puffy when we ate lunch. The lasagna was perfect, the cheese crispy and golden on top. Giggling and snorting and signing like mad, Dot was high as a kite, excited about her bowling party the following day, wondering what presents her friends would buy and looking forward to wearing the special bowling shoes.

"Do I get to keep them?" she signed.

Dad laughed. "No, silly! You have to give them back. But they're yours for two hours."

"Two whole hours?"

"Two whole hours," Dad repeated, tickling her chin.

"Kids," Mum whispered to Soph, whose face broke into a grin.

Now Stu you're probably wondering what was going on at Aaron's house, and believe me, I was thinking exactly the same thing, full of birthday cake, sprawled on the sofa as Mum and Dad had a long discussion in the kitchen. Who knows what they were going on about, but for once they weren't shouting so I could brood about the brothers in peace. Sort-of peace. If peace feels like pleasant pins and needles in your stomach. There was fear tingling in there. Excitement, too. For the hundredth

216

time, I checked my phone to find nothing but a picture of Dot as my screen saver, which she'd taken of herself without me knowing, sticking out her tongue with her eyes rolled backward, pushing up her nose so I could see inside her nostrils.

Nothing passed the time, not flicking through a magazine or writing *Bizzle the Bazzlebog* or tidying my room until even my DVDs were in alphabetical order. There was nothing left to do except crawl under my duvet and wait. I organized it like a tent over my head, blocking out the universe, and that's precisely where I was when my phone started ringing. I stared at the screen as Aaron's name lit up my world.

"Hey," I said, ridiculously pleased to hear from him.

"Hey," he replied in the opposite tone.

"How did it go? Was he mad? Did he punch you?" There was no response. "Oh God! He did, didn't he? Are you okay?"

Aaron exhaled noisily. "I was going to do it, I promise you."

"What do you mean, *was going to*? Didn't you say anything?"

"I couldn't, Zo. Honestly. We had to meet up with my dad. He was out with his girlfriend Tuesday so he asked to see us this afternoon instead. Had something important to tell us about her."

I closed my eyes, scared of where the conversation was heading. "Which was?"

"Put it this way, they aren't splitting up."

"She's pregnant?"

"Nope. They're getting married. He proposed on Valentine's Day. The wedding's in April."

"*April?* Isn't that a bit soon?"

217

"They don't see the point in waiting. You should have heard him," Aaron said, sounding revolted. "He's properly loved up."

"Are you okay?"

"I am, but Max . . . He managed to keep it in when we were with my dad, but when he got home, he threw a fit."

I pulled the duvet off my head, suddenly needing air. "We still have to tell him." Aaron didn't reply. Rolling onto my back, I stared at the ceiling with my hand on my forehead. "We can't hide this. Not after today. We *have* to tell him." The phone buzzed with the sound of nothing. "Aaron? Please say something."

"I'm sorry."

I swallowed, fear welling up inside me. "What do you mean?"

"He needs me, Zo. He needs you."

"But I can't pretend," I said, my eyes filling with tears. "I can't go into school on Monday and not mention what happened at the library."

"*Please*," Aaron begged. "Give us some time to think about what to do."

"Are you honestly saying you want me to walk up to him and kiss him and act like nothing's wrong?"

"I don't know. Look, can I see you tomorrow?" he asked, so I told him about Dot's party, and how I would have the house to myself for a few hours because Mum was making me stay behind to study for a science test. "I'll come over and we'll talk about it," he said. "We'll sort something out. I promise you."

"Okay."

There was silence for a while, and then the quietest of whispers.

"I don't regret it, Zo. Maybe I should, but I don't."

I gripped the phone. "Me, neither. Not one bit."

"Your voice changes when you smile."

I grinned even harder. "So does yours."

"This is messed up."

"Yeah."

"But we'll sort it out."

"I know."

"And then . . ."

"And then."

"S'long, Bird Girl."

"S'long."

The following day I was pretending to study my notes on magnetism when there was a knock on the door. Aaron was standing on my porch in a pair of blue jeans and a green hoodie, holding a tennis racket.

"Can I have my ball back, please?" he said like a small boy, and I did this daft girly sort of squeal, jumping into his arms, suddenly understanding the principles of magnetism a whole lot better than I ever had in class. "I still need my ball," Aaron said as I pulled him into my house. My house, Stu. Aaron was inside *my house*, his sneakers on my carpet, his smell mixing with Mum's polish.

"Did you actually throw a ball into my garden?"

"I hit one over your roof," Aaron said, pretending to serve and accidentally hitting the lamp shade with his racket.

We tore through the house, bursting into the back garden to

hunt for the ball. It became a competition, a mad race to be the first to find the ball, and we both spotted it at the exact same moment near a plant pot. With a spectacular dive, I grabbed it before Aaron did and sprinted off at top speed, cheering with the ball above my head. Aaron caught up with me, clutching my waist and lifting me high into the air.

"*All hail, Bird Girl!*" he announced, carrying me across the garden as I waved to my cheering fans, and then we both fell onto the wet grass. "Well done."

"Thank you," I replied, pretending to take a bow. We flopped onto our backs with our hands touching but not holding because there were rules that we had to obey and a conversation we had to have.

"So, what are we going to do?" Aaron asked, his voice becoming serious.

"Not yet," I groaned. "Not right now. Let's just lie here for a minute." Out of nowhere a bird burst into song, and I sat up, staring all around for the source of the noise.

"Swallow?" Aaron asked.

I giggled. "Just a house sparrow. The swallows are still in Africa. Probably having a crazy adventure." I lay back on the grass, and this time Aaron took my hand.

"That's what I'm going to do," Aaron said, squinting as the sparrow took off with a noise that sounded like freedom. "Travel the world."

"I'll go with you. When we've told Max and I've finished school and Mum can't stop me. I'll save up all my money from the library and we'll go to—"

"London? Manchester? Leeds?" Aaron teased. "Wouldn't get very far on your wages."

"You've got the money from your dad," I said. "You could take us both on an adventure."

Aaron pulled me onto his chest, my legs dangling between his as our hearts thumped on top of each other. "You're on," he whispered, his breath tickling my ear. "South America or somewhere." He pecked my forehead. And then my eyelids. And then my lips, opening his mouth, his tongue darting against mine. Pulling away, I waggled my finger in his face.

"Naughty! We're not supposed to be doing anything bad."

Aaron rolled on top of me, blocking out the sun.

"Sometimes there are good reasons to do bad things," he muttered. "Just ask Guy Fawkes."

"Cheesy."

"You love it!"

"I love you," I whispered, putting my hands on either side of his jaw and drawing him close, covering his face with tiny kisses, my lips finding the hard bridge of his nose and the soft fuzz of his eyebrows and the prickly stubble of his chin as he mouthed *me, too.*

The heavier things got, the lighter I felt until honest truth I was right up there with the sparrow, swooping and darting high above cloud nine. When it started to drizzle, Aaron pulled me to my feet and Stu we couldn't stop kissing, moving into the shed in a blur of mouths and hands and stumbling feet, stepping over tools and squeezing past the box of tiles, our actions growing more urgent as our love steamed up the windows and formed dew on the spiderwebs, glistening on the silk.

Aaron cleared a space in the junk and took Dad's old jacket off a peg, spreading it on the dusty floor. My fingers found the bottom of his hoodie, and I pulled it up, needing to see him to feel him to be close to his skin, and there it was, firm and smooth, and I stroked every last inch of it as he gasped without sound, his mouth opening as my thumb brushed the brown hair curling in soft spirals beneath his belly button.

He wrapped one hand around both of mine and raised my arms into the air, pulling my top over my head, my hair lifting up up up in the material then *swooshing* back down onto my bare shoulders. His eyes said *You're beautiful* and I felt it, too, as he took off my bra, slowly slowly, like he was scared of doing it wrong. Hardly breathing now, I pulled him down onto the coat, and we wrapped ourselves up in it as best we could, our bodies tangling together in a knot that no one could undo. My skin was on his skin, his body warmer than mine. He scooped his arm under my head. We blinked in unison. Inhaled the same air. And just as our lips were about to touch, there was a deafening

RING RING

RING RING

RING RING

Aaron reached into his back pocket, and I knew from his expression who was calling.

"Should I speak to him?" he asked, panic in his voice. Before I could reply, Max rang off. Dropping my head onto Aaron's arm, I exhaled loudly—only to breathe right back in again as my own phone buzzed in my pocket. "You'd better answer that, Zo."

"I can't!" I said, but I pressed a button anyway, leaning up on my elbow and turning away from Aaron.

We spoke, Stu, and I can barely write it down because Max was so upset about his dad's engagement and I was just trying to get him off the phone, muttering words I didn't mean as his brother lay next to me, his bare chest rising and falling as he listened to the conversation, his hands covering his eyes.

"What you up to, anyway?" Max asked eventually, and my throat tightened. I cleared it. Twice.

"Nothing much. Just studying for that science exam," I managed, and Aaron threw Dad's jacket to one side, standing up abruptly.

Max sighed through the phone. "I need to do some work for that. Do you want to come over? I've got the house to myself. Mum's out shopping with Fiona, and I don't know where my brother is."

I screwed up my face. "I should stay here," I said as Aaron pulled on his hoodie, yanking it over his head and shoving his arms through the sleeves. "Sorry. I have to concentrate."

"Please?" he said in a voice I didn't recognize. "I need to see you."

"Sorry," I said, apologizing for things he would never have believed. "I should go."

It took a while to get rid of him, and when I finally lowered the phone, I felt sick with shame.

"You did what you had to," Aaron said at last, but he was staring at the lawn mower rather than me, all the tenderness gone from his voice. "This is my fault," he muttered, sorting out his hair with jabbing fingers. "I should never have come."

"Don't say that. Please don't say that."

He sat down on the box of tiles, a look of self-loathing on his face. "What are we doing, Zoe? This is bad. This is really bad." Scrambling to my knees, I pressed my chest against his legs. Aaron put his hand on my bare back as I rested my head on his lap. "It can't happen again."

"I know."

"We have to tell him the truth."

I looked up at him. "Yeah. When, though?"

"I dunno. We have to wait for the right time, I guess."

"There is no right time," I whispered. "It's going to be awful whenever we do it. Horrible." He rubbed my shoulder as I started to cry, and I hated myself for being weak, but I couldn't stop the tears. "Let's wait till after the wedding at least. What you said on the phone yesterday. He needs you. And me. We can't—"

"But that's ages away, Zo."

We stared at each other helplessly. I sniffed, trying to be strong. "It's only a few weeks. A few weeks, that's all." I held his hands in mine, wiping my face with my arm. "We should set a date for telling him. I don't know. May first or something."

Aaron kissed my forehead. "All right. May first."

So that's how we decided, Stu, choosing the date at random, and I don't want to talk about what happened on that night, not now or ever. I don't want to talk about the rain or the trees or the disappearing hand or the blue sirens or the sobs or the lies or the coffin or the guilt the guilt the guilt that I feel every single minute of every single day. And if I have to write it all down, I want to do it in pencil so I can rub it straight back out again,

224

erasing that whole part of my life so it smudges into nothing and I can start again, drawing myself the way I want to be with a free smile and a pure heart and a name that I can write in block capitals because I'm not afraid to reveal it in a letter scribbled in a garden shed.

Love,
Zoe xxx
1 Fiction Road
Bath, UK

S. Harris #993765
Polunsky Unit (Death Row)
Livingston, Texas 77351
USA
April 12

My dear Stu,

By the time you receive this letter, you will be very near the
end, and I'm so sorry I couldn't do more to save you. All I can
hope is that the sun's shining on your last days, beaming through
your window as a red-tailed hawk soars in the sky. I hope it looks
different, the yellow brighter and the blue deeper and the scarlet feathers more vibrant than any you've ever seen in your life. I
wonder if you feel calm or if your heart's acting crazy. If you had
one of those hospital monitors, I wonder if it would go BOOM
BOOM BOOM like a giant's trapped inside it, or boom boom boom
boom boom as if a mouse is running through the wires.

Whatever is happening to that heart of yours, I hope it feels light and free as if it's going to drift right out of you toward the sun and float away into the universe when it finally stops beating. You deserve some happiness now, Stu. Of course you made mistakes, but you faced up to your crime and accepted your fate so at least your story ends bravely. With honesty. Mine ends differently, as you will see.

The morning of May 1 was perfect, like God had ironed a turquoise cloth across the sky and stitched a yellow circle right in the middle of it. It hurts to think how I closed my eyes to breathe in the day or how nice breakfast felt on the patio, Mum and Dad reading the newspaper and taking their time over a pot of real coffee, not talking much but not arguing over who got the business section, either. Soph was prancing on the lawn like a pony, making Dot helpless with laughter, and then they linked arms and galloped around the garden until Dot tripped. Of course, she blamed Soph, but Mum didn't run to Dot's side or put a Band-Aid on the graze. She just told her to be careful then went back to the paper as Dad smiled at something he was reading.

That night I was going to the Spring Fair in the park where the bonfire had been held. I couldn't sit still at breakfast or lunch or dinner, and I fidgeted away the hours, anticipating the moment I'd see Aaron. We'd kept our word and not met up, but we'd spoken on the phone practically every night, if you want me to be honest about it, sneaking a word here and there, checking in with each other, hating and loving the situation all at the same time, if that's even possible. The wedding had taken place in the last week of April so it was time to confess and we'd decided to do it together that evening. I put on my new blue dress, having a million practice conversations in my head, imagining Max saying *Don't worry* and smiling by the Ferris wheel.

At last it was time to set off so Dad drove into the city center, toward the stalls shining in the park underneath rows of flashing lights. He pulled up by a hot dog van. Onions sizzled. Smoke swirled. Music from two different live bands clashed in the air as rides zoomed by the river. I spotted Lauren making her way toward the park entrance so I jumped out of Dad's car and joined a large group that was growing by the second, families filing in from the left and the right. A clown was tottering about on stilts, giving out sweets, and Irish step dancers were doing something ridiculous that I can't even describe, and a brass band appeared in the middle of the street, all these marching black feet and farting gold instruments and musicians dressed in smart uniforms with brass buttons you could see your face in.

When I reached the gate, Lauren was clutching a metal spike, taking off a shoe, and flexing her toes.

"Too small?" I asked.

"Too small, too high, too tight, but *so* pretty!" she replied, stroking the red stiletto. "Let's go in!"

The sun started to set, and Stu it was spectacular, like imagine ice cream in a bowl, pink swirls and orange swirls and yellow swirls melting together to make colors that don't even have a name.

"Bumper cars?" Lauren suggested, so we paid to go on, but my heart wasn't really in it because I was looking looking looking for Aaron.

All of a sudden the bumper cars roared into life and everyone moved forward, but Lauren pressed the wrong pedal so we hurtled backward in a circle. Round and round and round we went, both our mouths wide open and screaming. When we finally got ourselves going in the right direction, a boy came out of nowhere and smashed into the back of the car, jolting us forward. I swore under my breath, realizing with a shock that it was Max. Guilt and anger mixed in my stomach as he reversed quickly. Putting his foot probably flat on the floor, he charged toward us once more and crashed into our side.

"*Stop it!*" Lauren shouted as our heads snapped forward. Jack yelled something—he was there, too, speeding around in a fluorescent yellow car—and Max threw back his head and guffawed as Lauren, furious, hit the wrong pedal again so we shot backward into a pillar.

When the ride finished, I climbed out of the bumper car on shaky legs. I wanted more than anything to disappear in the opposite direction, but Max grabbed my arm.

"That was a bit much, Max," Lauren said, rubbing her neck. He shrugged, his eyes wild as he leaned in with no warning, his teeth clattering against my top lip. His breath tasted of vodka and onions as he sucked my face, no other way to describe it.

"*Gross*," Lauren muttered, which was the exact word I was thinking as I pushed him away.

"I'm only *celebrating!*"

"Celebrating what?"

"Weddings!" Max yelled, raising his arms into the air. "Marriage!"

Just as Lauren twirled a finger by her temple to say that Max had clearly gone mental, the boy in the year above grabbed her around the waist and pulled her toward the bumper cars. Stumbling in high heels, Lauren climbed into a pink one, and I watched her speed around as Jack handed Max a bottle of clear liquid. He gulped down a mouthful and passed it back. Jack put the bottle on a bench, looking queasy. All the lights from the fair shone in the glass and I gazed at it, thinking it was beautiful, then turned my head to see Aaron.

My eyes lit up in recognition, my expression overfamiliar and my voice about to give us away. Aaron shook his head quickly before Max could see. I changed my face. Kept it calm. But underneath my skin, excitement bubbled in my blood. It was almost our time, Stu. Almost.

"Aaron!" Max exclaimed. "Zoe, this is my brother. The best brother in the world, and that's not even a lie. You should have seen him at the wedding." His words were slurring, and he patted Aaron on the back so hard he stumbled forward.

"We've already met," Aaron muttered as I cringed all the way from my curling toes to the prickling roots of my hair. "Remember?"

"Noooo," Max replied, and then he started to giggle in this false sort of way, holding his own arms and moving his shoulders up and down. "'Course I remember. New Year's Eve.

Me and Zoe were going to"—he dropped his voice to a whisper—"*you know* in your car." Max held out a fist and a finger and put one inside the other, pumping hard. Sweat crept up my back, crawling underneath my arms and breaking into hot beads on my upper lip. Aaron looked away as Max's hands reached a climax that splattered into the air between all three of us. He winked at me. "Maybe later." His crooked smile looked dangerously off-kilter as he put an arm around my shoulder and held me close.

That's when Sandra emerged out of the crowd.

"Look at you two," she said, smiling at us all indulgent as Max kissed my cheek, leaving spit on my skin. My shoulder twitched because I wanted to wipe it off, but I let it dry, this sticky ring right in the middle of my face, and I remember feeling branded. "It's boiling, isn't it?" Sandra said, fanning herself, her hair sticking to her forehead. "How're you, Zoe?"

"Good, thanks," I lied, my voice strained. Aaron's fists were clenching because Max's hand had found my hair, twirling a strand between his fingers.

"You soppy thing." Sandra laughed, tapping Max's shoulder and beaming with pride as her youngest son gazed at me with all this affection that was more vodka than anything, not that Sandra realized it.

There wasn't much oxygen, because of the panic or the humidity, and I had to work hard to suck air into my lungs. A silver balloon bobbed above the crowd and moved toward us as Fiona appeared with the blue string tied around her hand, her camera dangling from her neck.

"Zoe!" she cried, running up to me in a flowery dress. "You haven't been to our house for ages."

"Every time I ask, she's busy," Max sulked.

"You must come over more often," Sandra said, dabbing her forehead with a tissue as the sun sank below the horizon, turning the sky into that inky sort of blue that comes before the black. "You're welcome anytime, sweetheart."

Aaron sucked his cheek between his back teeth, white grinding on red.

"Take a picture of us," Max said, prodding Fiona's tummy with his finger.

"*Ow!*"

"Go on," he said. "All three of us!" He pulled me and Aaron into a space away from the crowd, forcing me into the middle. Fiona fiddled with the settings as Aaron's arm snaked around my back, his hand squeezing my hip as we glanced at each other with blazing eyes bursting with all the things we couldn't say and all the feelings we weren't supposed to have, and I ached for him—for his voice and his smell and his touch and his taste and his . . .

"*Smile!*" Fiona shouted, so I turned on a big grin that disappeared with the zap of the flash.

At the other side of the bumper cars, Lauren waved at me to say she was disappearing with the boy in the year above. Black clouds had appeared above the woods near the river, heat pressing down pressing down pressing down.

"There's going to be a storm." Sandra frowned, rubbing her temples, and sure enough a jagged stripe of silver cut through the dense air, tearing the sky in two. "I'm going to get off," she said quickly. "You lot can get wet if you like, but I'm taking Fiona home."

"*No*," Fiona groaned, stamping her foot. "I haven't been on the ghost train yet!"

"Tough," Sandra said as—*pt pt pt*—the first drops of rain splattered the ground. Pulling a jacket out of her bag, Sandra told Max and Aaron that she would pick them up in a couple of hours, and Stu it hurts to remember how casually she said this, as if there was just no question that the brothers would be waiting at the hot dog van at 11:30 PM. She hurried off, distracted by the rain, without stopping to kiss her sons.

And then there were three.

Lightning flashed as if the tension between us was exploding in the sky. Max picked up the bottle of vodka Jack had left on the bench.

"Don't you think you've had enough?" Aaron said, but Max's mouth bulged and his throat contracted as he gulped down the clear liquid. He smacked his lips apart.

"I'm celebrating!" He lifted the bottle over his head then stumbled off through the crowd, calling over his shoulder, "Just *celebrating* the wedding!" Aaron and I exchanged a worried look, and even though it was wrong, we smiled a bit, too. "Fiona had the right idea," Max said, suddenly spinning around. Our grins vanished just in time. "Let's go on the ghost train!"

BANG!

Thunder!

People screamed as the rain doubled in force, pelting out

of the sky. Umbrellas shot into the air. Everyone dived for cover underneath roofs dripping with water. Only Max charged through the downpour, slipping and sliding on the mud as he joined the shrinking queue at the ghost train. Shielding my eyes from the rain, I followed, struggling to keep up with Aaron.

"This is ridiculous!" I shouted at Max as he swigged the vodka again and again. "We need to find somewhere to go inside!"

"That's inside!" he yelled, pointing at the ghost train and gulping back more drink. Aaron tried to take the bottle, but Max shoved him, harder than he intended, the heel of his hand smacking against Aaron's shoulder.

"Easy, Max."

"*Easy, Max*," his brother mocked, knocking back another mouthful as we reached the front of the queue. Pushing the bottle down the back of his jeans, Max leaped into the carriage, disappearing through purple doors as a ghost wailed.

"We can't tell him tonight!" I exclaimed, my hair dripping wet as rain beat down from the jet-black sky. "He's totally out of it!"

"I know! We'll wait. Tomorrow, though," Aaron said, and our hands touched for the slightest moment as Max's carriage shot out of an arch on the upper level. Our fingers broke apart as Max waved madly, hurtling through the gaping mouth of a huge ghost painted on the opposite side of the ride. It was my turn next so Aaron helped me into my carriage. Off I went, following Max with Aaron just behind, through tunnels that spun, under spiderwebs that tickled my face, past monsters that roared and coffins that opened, the wheels of the carriage clacking on the metal track.

"I feel sick," Max moaned as I climbed out of my carriage into the rain, shivering now, my blue dress stuck to my skin. "You look amazing," he said, his words slurring badly. Gently, he brushed my wet fringe to one side then his face drained of color. "I'm going to throw up." He bent over, his head dangling above a puddle. I put my hand on his back. "Don't," he muttered.

"There's a trash can over there," I said, pointing, but Max stumbled toward the woods as Aaron's carriage sped out of the ghost train.

I gestured at the trees to tell Aaron where I was heading so I could follow Max, worried about him falling as he ran away from the fair, unsteady on his legs. Squinting in the darkness, I hurried away from the crowds, going deeper and deeper into the woods, mud squelching beneath my feet. I didn't know if Aaron was behind me, but I could see Max in front, tripping over a trunk to land on the grass.

It can't have hurt, but Max didn't get up. Rain dripped through branches. The noise of the fair was muffled by the gushing of a river I couldn't see. I dropped to my knees at Max's side.

"Go away," he said, and I realized with dismay that he was crying. "I'm celebrating, Zo. *Celebrating!*" Gently, I put my fingers on his head, and it seemed to calm him. Slowly, he turned to look at me, sweat and mud and tears mingling on his cheeks. He sat up suddenly, forcing his lips on mine.

"Don't," I said, scrambling to my feet, unable to control my reaction.

"Why not?" Max slurred, wiping his face with his sleeve. He jumped up to kiss me again, clutching my arms. "Don't be shy, Zo." Straining my neck to look over Max's shoulder, I saw nothing but trees, the lights of the fair this speck of color in the distance. I'd come farther than I'd realized.

"I don't want to," I said as Max slurped at my neck, his breath quivering against my skin.

"You're my girlfriend," he whispered, and the guilt was so strong my legs almost gave way. "Come on...." His mouth was on mine before I could stop it, his hands grabbing my bum before darting to the front to push inside my knickers.

"Stop it," I said, struggling to get free. Max laughed, tickling my sides, then under my arms, then touching my breasts, not hard, more pathetically than anything, but my heart was pounding. "Seriously, Max. I don't want to."

"You'll enjoy it," he crooned, moving his fingers all over my body as I squirmed, biting my bottom lip, desperate not to hurt his feelings, but Stu he was scaring me, pulling at the strap of my dress as I shook my head. "What's wrong with you?" he asked, sounding annoyed now, and he grabbed both straps and tore them down. "You're my girlfriend, aren't you?" he yelled, and that's when I pushed him away and took off, unable to stand it a second longer.

"Zoe!" Max called, his voice bouncing off the trees as I ran back toward the fair. "Zoe! I'm sorry. We don't have to do anything you don't... *Come back! Zoe!*"

I turned to see him sink to his knees with his head in his hands, and I pushed forward, frightened and exhausted and sick to death of pretending. Panting, I stumbled toward Aaron, who had entered the woods.

"Hey," he said, his voice full of concern. "What's the matter, Zo? What is it?"

"Max," I gasped, shaking as I fell into his arms. "He's . . . he's . . ."

"He's what?" Aaron asked, holding my face in his hands, kissing me with all the desperation that we both felt, giving in for a frantic second because it was dark, so dark, and we were hidden under the trees.

But then a twig snapped.

We spun around to see the back of Max's head as he hurtled into the woods. For a moment, neither of us moved, and then we leaped apart, horrified, calling out his name, chasing after him, the sound of gushing water getting louder and louder as we pushed past branches and tore at leaves and slipped on the mossy ground. The river appeared as the trees gave way to a stony path and I skidded to a halt, looking all around, my lungs on fire. Max was stumbling along it, losing his footing again and again, his feet dangerously close to the surging water.

"*Max!*" Aaron yelled, his hands on either side of his mouth. "*MAX!*"

If Max heard, he gave no sign of it. I turned to Aaron, my face white, my eyes huge and terrified.

"He saw us! He knows! What are we going to—"

But Aaron had sped off again, struggling to run in his

flip-flops as they flicked mud up the back of his jeans. *"Max!"* he called. *"Max!"*

Max stopped abruptly, his attention caught by a wooden bench. Roaring in anger, he picked up a stone, and I realized with a sickening jolt what he'd seen—our initials, Stu, scratched into the wood. Raising the stone above his head, he dived at the bench, and just as he was about to attack our names, Aaron seized his arm.

"I'm sorry," he said. "I'm so sorry!"

My feet splashed through puddles as the black river swirled, and both boys turned to look at me.

"What's going on?" Max roared, throwing the stone against the bench. "What the *F* is going on?"

"We . . . we . . ." I stuttered, my hands clawing at my hair.

"We're . . ." Aaron started.

"You're *WHAT*?" Max yelled, tears falling down his face. "What's going on? *TELL ME THE TRUTH!*"

Aaron held up his hands. "Calm down," he breathed. "Calm down! We'll talk about this when you've sobered up and everyone's—"

"Don't tell me what to do!" Max bellowed, slapping Aaron's hand away. "You bastard!" Aaron sank onto the bench. "You're all I've got!" Max said, his voice choked. He tripped over nothing, almost falling onto Aaron's lap. "And *you*," he growled, rounding on me, his movements huge and lurching as he swiped an arm through the air. "I trusted you. I *liked* you!"

"I liked you, too! I swear . . . I never meant for any of this to happen." I tried to put my hands on his waist to comfort him, but he pushed me away and I stumbled toward the river.

"Don't talk to me, you slut!"

Aaron shot to his feet. "Don't call her that!"

Laughing crazily now, Max hurtled toward me. The water churned half a meter from where we stood. Grabbing my shoulder, he pulled me upright to shout in my ear.

"SLUT!"

"Stop!" Aaron yelled. "Leave her out of this!"

"Don't tell me what to do!" Max screamed again as thunder exploded in the sky. He gripped the straps of my blue dress with desperate fingers, and we wobbled closer to the river.

"Let her go!" Aaron bellowed, and when Max didn't obey, Aaron charged at his brother. They came together with an almighty roar, gripping each other as their feet slipped on the mud.

"You're too near the edge!" I cried, but they weren't listening, and somehow I got in the middle, trying to break them up as they grasped each other's clothes, shoving and pushing and screaming underneath the trees as the rain pelted down.

"You *slut*!" Max bellowed, spit hitting my skin as he grabbed my hair and roared the word in my face, and Stu I pushed him hard as Aaron did, too. A split-second impulse. Anything to make him stop.

His feet skidded down the wet bank. The slippery slope.

His arms propelled madly in the air.

And the water splashed as his body fell in, his mouth opening at the first shock of cold.

"Get him!" I screamed. "Aaron! Grab him!"

Paralyzed to the spot, I watched Aaron drop onto his chest and hold out his hand as the strong current grabbed Max's legs,

239

swirling and powerful, impossible to fight. As if in slow motion, I saw Max go under—once, twice—his body sweeping down the river as Aaron scrambled along the bank, gasping and shouting, stretching out his arm.

Max couldn't reach it. The river was too strong. As he struggled to swim against the current, his muscles went limp and he floated passed tree roots and branches and an orange safety ring on the other side of the river that none of us could reach. He went under again, and again and again, getting weaker and weaker, his mouth sucking in water as he struggled to kick himself above the surface.

Aaron stretched out one last time, shouting his brother's name. Max lifted a weak arm into the air as his body gave up the fight.

His head sank.

His elbow, too.

Wrist.

Hand.

The disappearing hand—pale and rigid and grasping at nothing—vanished under the black water.

The first time we lied was to the operator on the other end of the phone. Aaron called for an ambulance, and even though he was shaking and sobbing, he didn't mention the argument or the kiss or our push.

"He slipped," Aaron said, sitting on the bench, his body shaking violently. "He was drunk." I gazed at him as he hung up, unable to protest because my voice wouldn't work. Curled up in a ball on the side of the river, I started to rock, and I didn't stop until somehow Mum and Dad appeared at my side and a police officer threw a blanket over my shoulders as Sandra screamed into the night.

The next few hours were a blur of questions in a gray station that smelled of photocopiers and coffee. In a small room on a hard chair, I just kept saying the same thing over and over again, latching on to Aaron's words. *Max slipped. He was drunk. He slipped. He was drunk.* At some point the police officer must have believed me because he told me I was free to go home.

Only it wasn't home. It was a building I didn't recognize, with a family that was a group of strangers. My room wasn't my room, and my bed wasn't my bed, because I wasn't me. I was someone else, a stranger who my parents didn't know. A cheat. A liar. A killer. I lay under a duvet that smelled of the life I'd lost, and looked at my hands, blinking in shock.

I ended up in the bath the next morning. Mum ran it for me. She put this salt stuff in the water that was supposed to be good for trauma. I'd never had a bath at 10 AM before. It felt odd. Too light in the bathroom. Sun shone through the window and dust motes swirled above the laundry basket. Water dripped from the hot tap, and I put my toe in the hole but couldn't feel it burn.

That afternoon, Dad came into my room.

"The boy's mum invited you over, pet. Sandra, I think her name is."

I started to count.

One. Two. Three. Four. Five.

"The rest of Max's family is there," Dad said, sitting on my bed. "I think it's important that you see them."

Six. Seven. Eight.

"Pet, are you listening?"

"Yes."

"What do you think?"

"About what?" I muttered.

Dad's face clouded over and he held my hand. "Going to Max's house? I'll come with you if you like. It might help to be around other people."

Nine. Ten. Eleven.

"Anyway. I'll leave it with you," Dad said, standing up as I stared at the ceiling, my face completely still.

I watched a neighbor mow his lawn and plant six shrubs. I watched a man paint his windows and his front door. I watched a dog go for a walk and come back carrying a stick.

Next morning, Mum came into my room and told me I had a temperature. She said my glands were swollen and told me to open my mouth, shining a flashlight down my throat as I said, "*Aaaaaaaaah.*" She turned off the beam and told me I could stop, but I kept on saying it louder and louder.

aaaaaaaaaaaaaaaaaaaaaaaahhhhhhhhhhhhhhhhhhhhhhhhhh-
hhhhhhhhhhhhhhhhhhhhhhhhhhhhhhhhhhhhhhhhhhhhhhhhh-
hhhhhhhhhhhhhhhhhhhhhhhhhhhhhhhhhhhhhhhhhhhhhhhhh-
hhhhhhhhhhhhhhhhhhhhhhhhhhhhhhhhhhhhhhhhhhhhhhhhh-
hhhhhhhhhhhhhhhhhhhhhhhhhhhhhh

"Has Zoe gone mental?" Dot signed.

My mouth snapped closed.

"No," Mum said. "She's just upset."

Dot looked at me warily. "I don't do that when I'm upset."

242

"It's a very big upset," Mum explained. "Bigger than you've had before."

"Because of the boyfriend?"

"Yes."

"I didn't know she had one of those," Dot signed.

"Me, neither, my love. Not really. But I do know he made her happy." Mum stroked my forehead as Aaron's name burned on my lips. The heat of it turned my cheeks scarlet, and Stu in that moment I wanted Mum to ask what was wrong, but she just moved her thumb over my eyebrow, muttering, "She was glowing when I picked her up from the library."

"Why did he drown?" Dot asked.

Mum glanced at me before replying. "I don't know."

"Because if he could swim then why did he sink? And I also have another question."

"That's enough now."

"Can I have the day off school as well?"

More days passed in pretty much the same blur. Mum brought food. Dad provided endless cups of tea. By the time Dot got home from school one afternoon later that week, I had six mugs lined up on my bedside table, full of different amounts of liquid. I tapped them all with a pen to make music.

"When's the funeral going to be and do I get to go?" I shut my eyes so I didn't have to watch her words. She peeled back my lids with her chubby fingers. "I said, when's the funeral going to be and do I get to go and also do the important people walk behind the coffin and am I one of them or do I just have to wait in the church?"

Dad knocked softly on my door.

"Dot, dinner's ready," he signed.

"I'm not hungry."

"It's waiting for you on the table."

"I'm too upset about the boy to eat. My teacher said I've got *grief*."

"If you're grieving, perhaps I should tell your mum it's time for you to go to bed."

Dot's eyes widened, and she sprinted out of my room at top speed. Dad sighed.

"She's a funny one." The mattress squeaked as he sat down. "I just got off the phone, pet. Sandra called again. She wanted me to tell you they're burying him on Friday."

I turned away and stared at the wall. Dad put his hand into my hair and we stayed like that for ages, and I wish he were here right now to rub my head and tell me it will be fine and to be strong because the feelings will pass. I want them to go now, Stu. I'm ready for them to disappear, and I know you're the same, tired of the pain and the fear and the sadness and the guilt and the hundred other feelings that don't even have a name in all of the English language.

There's one more letter to write before we both can stop. One more about the funeral and the wake and finding out from Sandra that Aaron had set off on a last-minute trip to South America without bothering to say good-bye to me. Because it will be the last, maybe we should do something special to celebrate. Perhaps we should have a final meal, which for me would be steak and fries, and we could eat together, you on one side of the ocean and me on the other, a sparkling blue tablecloth spanning the distance between us. Candles would flicker in the sky, and once and for all I'd finish my tale. You would be satisfied and I would be content so we'd both blow out the flames. You, me, the shed, the cell, our stories, our secrets—all of it would disappear, hovering in the darkness like smoke before fading to nothing.

Love always,

Zoe xxx

1 Fiction Road

Bath, UK

S. Harris #993765

Polunsky Unit (Death Row)

Livingston, TEXAS 77351

USA

May 6

My dearest Stu,

I came back when I promised to. I don't want you to think I
didn't return like we'd discussed. Honest truth I told you
everything, just as we'd planned. I described how Aaron's face
had fallen in on itself as he'd lifted the coffin at the start of
the procession. I told you how his hands had shaken beneath the
weight of his brother and how that Morning really had felt
Broken into a million little pieces that could never be fixed. I
said how I'd been introduced to every single relative as Max's
girlfriend and how Aaron hadn't looked at me once during
the wake and how Soph had made a lame joke about how
inappropriate it is for a wake to be called a wake when the

guest of honor can't even be bothered to open his eyes.

I explained how Lauren had visited me later that day, giving me the red stilettos to cheer me up, and how she'd flicked through all the sympathy cards on a pile by my bed. I described how she'd sniggered at one that said *Taken by God because he was too good for this earth*, telling you how she'd muttered "Too good for this earth? If Max is in heaven, I bet he's trying to F an angel."

So, yeah, I told you pretty much everything, and then I put that letter in an envelope, sealing it up to take to the post office the following morning to reach you before May 1, just like I'd always planned.

Next day, I shoved it in my pocket and went to tell Mum I was going for a walk. She was sitting in the living room, sipping a cup of tea, taking a break from the chores as rain splattered on the windows.

"You want to go out in this?"

"Need some air," I muttered, very aware of the envelope in my jeans. I yawned because I'd been up late writing in the shed.

"Are you okay, Zoe?" she asked suddenly, and Stu the way she said it made my stomach drop.

"Fine," I replied, trying to smile as the letter in my pocket seemed to double in weight.

Dot sprinted into the living room waving the American flag because she's grown out of her Queen phase. Now she's decided to be the first female, first English American president, making laws like no more war and free banana ice cream for everyone. Climbing onto the piano stool, she stood with her hand on her heart as if she were listening to the American national anthem.

Watching her, Mum opened her mouth, closed it again, hesitated for a while, and then started to speak.

"I want . . . Look, I need to tell you something, Zoe."

"But I'm about to go out."

"It's my fault."

"What is?" I asked. Mum gestured at Dot, who was waving the flag from side to side. "It's your fault she's . . ."

"Deaf. It's okay, you can say it."

"But . . . I thought . . . Wasn't she born that way? That's what you and Dad have always said."

Mum shook her head, gazing at her knees. "When I got pregnant with her, it was an accident."

"*Mum.*"

"I didn't want to have her," Mum continued without looking at me or pausing for breath. "I was happy with two daughters, but your dad convinced me. Grandpa, too, for that matter." I sat down on the floor next to her feet, completely stunned. "Dad confided in him, saying I was thinking of getting rid of it."

"An abortion?" Mum put her finger over her lips, even though Dot couldn't hear a thing.

"It didn't go down too well, what with Grandpa being religious. They ganged up on me, I suppose you could say. We'd just lost Gran, and they told me how nice it would be to have a new life in the family. A baby. They really pressured me into it."

"Is that why . . . I mean, in your jewelry box you've got all my baby stuff, and Soph's, too, but nothing from Dot."

Mum shrugged sadly, her fingers clasped around her mug. "I struggled to bond with her. Resented her a little bit, if I'm being completely honest. I couldn't wait to go back to work." Dot leaped off the piano stool, the flag flying behind her like a cape. "One day, when she was only a few months old, she woke up with a temperature. I was annoyed because I had a big meeting at work and I was supposed to be delivering a presentation to a new client. I convinced myself it was nothing to worry about. Nothing serious." Her voice was barely louder than a whisper now. "I left her with the nanny, and when I got into the office, I turned off my phone so that I could focus. My secretary had to tell me she'd been taken to the hospital. Do you remember?"

I nodded slowly. "Just little bits. A tiny bed. Lots of tubes. I didn't really know what was wrong with her. You never said."

Mum brought her cup to her mouth but didn't sip her tea. "Meningitis. The doctors managed to save her, but they couldn't do anything about the damage to her hearing."

Dot ran out of the room, the flag wafting at her side. We both watched her go.

"I blamed myself for a long time. A very long time. Grandpa did, too. That's what he said to me in the heat of the moment. Accused me of being a bad mother. Not wanting Dot in the first place then abandoning her when she was ill. I couldn't forgive him, though it wasn't really him I hated, of course." She looked straight at me then, and Stu I blushed under the intensity of her gaze. "Guilt like that—it destroys a person. You have to find a way to let it go." She widened her eyes, glancing meaningfully out of the back window toward the shed, and I thought suddenly of the woolly hat and scarf and the deck chair and the blanket. "Whatever it is, you have to let it go. It's hard, Zoe. But you have to forgive yourself."

Mum went back to her tea as I stood up, but when I reached the hall, I didn't turn toward the front door. I wandered into the kitchen. Slowly, I took the last letter out of my pocket, the end of my story, and threw it in the trash.

This one's a little different, Stu. For one thing, I'm not writing it in the shed. I'm at my desk in my bedroom, and it's the middle of the day, not the middle of the night. I know you'll never read it—I know you can't now—but I wanted to share something with you anyway. Who knows, maybe if there are such things as spirits, you're floating there all transparent, peering over my shoulder, keen to find out what happened at the memorial service on May 1.

I finally got a reading together, finding something perfect at the very last second. I paced up and down my room all day, practicing my words, wondering if Aaron would be at the service or if he was still in South America, sitting on a beach, thinking about his mum and his brother and the trees and the rain and the disappearing hand. Sandra had told me that he would try to make it, but she wasn't hopeful and neither was I.

"It's a long way to come," she'd said a couple of weeks before. "Very expensive. I don't think he can afford it."

Of course, Aaron wasn't the only thing on my mind that day. You were there, too, Stu, sitting in your cell. Ready. Accepting. Brave. I knew the execution was going to happen at 6 PM in Texas, midnight in England. York, in case you're wondering. Fulstone Avenue, not Fiction Road. I guess there's no reason to keep that a secret anymore.

The memorial service was due to start at 6 PM English time. I filled the long hours by inventing American laws with Dot, and Stu you'll be pleased to know we abolished capital punishment and improved prisons by giving them decorations at Christmas and guards who share pizza and nice big windows that you can see the whole sun right out of.

"You okay, pet?" Dad asked when I finally came downstairs in my black dress.

"Of course she's not," Mum said. "But she will be." Her eyes were fierce and they gave me strength as Dot hurtled out of the coat closet. I could barely see her face underneath a black hat.

"You don't have to wear every item of black clothing that you possess," Dad signed, opening the front door.

"But I didn't get to go to the funeral last year," Dot replied, smoothing down her black skirt with her black gloves. "I'm making up for it."

"At least take off the scarf," Mum signed.

"And the eye patch," Soph added, reaching over to pull it off Dot's face.

When we arrived at the school, the reception area was crowded. Coat stands were bending under the weight of so many black jackets. Faces looked pale above so many black tops.

The bulletin board was crammed full of pictures of Max, and in the center of it all was the photo of the three of us at the Spring Fair. If you looked closely, you could tell. I might have been standing in the middle of the brothers, but my body was turned slightly toward Aaron, and his knuckles were white as his fingers gripped my hip.

Lauren burst onto the scene with bright pink lips, a sudden speck of color in all the gloom.

"How're you doing?" she asked.

"Not good."

"Me, neither," she muttered. "Fifteen quid for this. The funeral was free."

A lady in a long black cardigan swooped on us like a crow, her hand clutching a tissue even though her eyes were dry.

"You're Max's girlfriend, aren't you?" she asked in a shaky voice.

I started to nod, but Lauren butted in. "No. Max is dead. Her name's Alice. Alice Jones," she said, because Stu that's what I'm really called.

The lady looked shocked then flew off to find her place at one of the tables. There were loads of them spilling out of the school hall, and one larger table on a stage at the front next to a microphone stand. My heart lurched when I spotted it, and I felt anxiously for the reading in my pocket.

It was almost time. Mouth dry, I walked toward the hall, and that's when I saw him.

You know who, Stu.

He was standing in the middle of the room like he'd never

been away, and I drank drank drank in the sight of him as if my eyes had been dying of thirst for months. His hair was longer and his skin was tanned, but his smile was the same. Despite everything, it flickered on his lips as I lifted my hand to wave.

"He came after all," Sandra said in my ear, making me jump. "Turned up this morning as a surprise."

Walking on air—maybe even flying—I made my way into the hall, right to the very front, sinking onto a chair at the end of the main table. Aaron climbed onto the stage, too, and found his seat at the opposite end, rearranging his knife and fork so they were perfectly straight.

The microphone screeched with feedback. Sandra backed away from it, her notes trembling in her hand. She waited an instant. Approached it once more. She said how wonderful it was that we were all together to celebrate Max's life. Aaron stared at his spoon. She said what a difficult year it had been for all of us. I stared at my spoon. She said that Max was gone but not forgotten and that he'd been such a wonderful son, a fantastic brother, a lovely boyfriend—and that's when I looked at Aaron and he looked at me, and Stu the sadness I felt in the most secret part of me was written all over his face.

"And now I'd like to ask Max's girlfriend to speak," Sandra said. Members of the audience exchanged sympathetic looks. Every single pair of eyes in the room was fixed on me, apart from the pair I actually cared about.

Aaron was gazing at his napkin.

I didn't move from my seat.

Fiona nudged me in the ribs.

I still didn't budge.

"It's your turn," Sandra mouthed.

My chair scraped backward. My heels echoed on the floor. Slowly slowly I pulled the poem out of my pocket. Your poem, actually, Stu. The one you wrote in the last week of your life.

"Release."

My stomach was a knot, and somewhere in Texas, I knew yours was, too. I reached the microphone and unfolded the words. Your words. The knot in my stomach tightened, and Stu the connection between us felt taut and painful but something to hold on to, thick as rope.

Ready.

Accepting.

Brave.

When I started to read, my voice was surprisingly calm. The words were clear. I stood up a little taller, spoke even louder, saying the poem not for Max or Sandra or anyone else in that room. Not even for Aaron. I said it for you and I said it for me—for our stories and our mistakes and your end and maybe even my beginning.

The memorial was a success even if the spotted dick was cold. As I tried to leave the school, everyone swarmed around me, telling me how wonderful the reading had been.

"I felt Max," someone said, pressing their chest, "in here."

"Did you see the lights flicker when she finished the poem? That was him."

"I heard the radiator groan in the first verse. I reckon that was him, too."

Mum gave me my coat and led me outside, away from the crowd, where I could breathe more easily. Before I could reach the car, I felt a hand on mine. I didn't have to turn around to know whose it was.

"Do you want to get out of here, Bird Girl?"

I told Mum I was going to Lauren's. I don't know if she believed me, but she didn't ask any questions, just gave me a quick hug and shouted at Dot for waving the American flag so hard she almost blinded a pensioner.

DOR1S seemed to purr when Aaron started the engine, as if she was pleased we were back. We didn't speak, just drove out of the city into the countryside on our way to absolutely nowhere, and when we found that perfect spot among some trees, we stopped and looked at each other. We knew without a word that nothing could happen, but Aaron spread his coat on the grass and we sat next to each other to watch the sun go down. Swallows swooped through the red sky, back from their adventure, and we held each other underneath the ketchup clouds, willing time to stop and the world to forget us for a while.

There's nothing much more to say. Eventually, Aaron dropped me off next to the Chinese takeout, and our tears glowed green as the emerald dragon roared in silent protest.

"So long, Bird Girl," he whispered, changing the emphasis to stress the first word.

"So long," I agreed, because a life without him would be.

I didn't go straight home. I went to the river for the first time since Max died. The moon glistened on the water as I fingered the initials scratched into the wood.

MM + AJ
Feb 14

I grabbed a stone and knelt by the bench as somewhere on the other side of the world, you lay down for the last time. A clock struck midnight as I began to scrape my initials off the wood. It wasn't done hard or furiously or through tears. It was quite calm. Gentle almost. But Stu it was good to see them fade.

Yours truly,
ALICE JONES

Bird Girl.

Blame the parrot for this letter. At least I think it's a parrot. Being a bird nonexpert, it's difficult to tell. If you were here, you'd laugh in that way of yours and say, "Parrot?! Aaron, it's a..."

Wow.

My ornithological knowledge is so poor I can't even think of another bird with multicolored wings that might be kept in a cage for the amusement of the customers. Not this customer, though. Oh no. This customer can no longer look at a bird behind bars without thinking of a certain girl with a certain love of the sound of freedom.

I'm in a town called Rurrenabaque in Bolivia, having a

drink. Perhaps you're imagining me sipping beer from a gnarled keg in a makeshift bar on a long stretch of gold beach, surrounded by locals. Well, let me set you straight: I'm sitting on an ordinary plastic chair behind an ordinary plastic table by an ordinary busy road, and two drunk English guys are having a competition to see who can burp the alphabet. It's quite the spectator sport. Mr. Stubble just got to the letter F before Mr. Bald reached the dizzy heights of N. N! In one belch! No wonder they're cheering.

Watching them, I swear to God I could be back in York. It was the same in Ecuador, no matter where I went. Even during a trek in the remotest part of the Andes, stuff felt familiar. Take this family who agreed to let me stay for a couple of days. Walking into their hut in the middle of the mountains, I thought they were different at first. The people wore a style of clothes I had never seen before and spoke this strange language, not even Spanish. There was no Internet, no electricity even, so no way of knowing what was going on in the world, and that was fine by me.

My bed was a heap of rugs in the corner of a drafty room, and as I dropped my backpack onto the floor and looked out of the window, I saw a woman kill a chicken with her bare hands. She'd done it thousands of times, I could tell, holding the chicken upside down and snapping its neck as she laughed at a baby who was playing with a stone at her side. Now, it's possible that chickens aren't birds in the way that spiders aren't insects, but either way I bet you're pretty much appalled. I was, too, don't get me wrong, but I was glad to feel horrified. Here was something so far from my experience, my jaw actually dropped. Home felt a million miles away. Mum. Max. You. You all sort of faded away, which is what I needed because remembering hurt too much.

But then this baby with the reddest cheeks I've ever seen pulled himself up to standing by holding on to his mum's skirt. He was wobbly, his chubby legs unsteady. His mum dropped the chicken and crouched down, gently taking the baby's hands. Shuffling backward, she helped the baby walk, and she was grinning and the baby was grinning and then the dad appeared and he was grinning, talking excitedly with his wife. Of course, I couldn't understand the words, but I knew full well what they were saying.

Look at him go! Can you believe it? Oops, be careful! Who's a clever little boy?

The baby tottered right into his mother's arms and she held him tightly as the man kissed the top of both their heads before going inside, and my stomach ached with disappointment at the familiarity of it all. Humans. We're all the same. There's no escaping it. Doesn't matter if you're a bald English guy burping the alphabet or a woman killing chickens in the middle of the Andes. Doesn't matter what language you speak or what clothes you wear. Some things don't change. Families. Friends. Lovers. They're the same in every city in every country in every continent of the world.

I want you to take your place among them, Bird Girl. You— the most exuberant, most vibrant, most beautiful person I know, the girl who writes about Bazzlebogs and makes happiness out of croissants—deserve to live. The day I left for South

America, I came to the library to see you. Who knows what I was going to say, but when I got there and saw you stacking shelves, I decided against it. Your back was to me, but I could tell you were upset. Your movements said it all, the way you lifted the books as if they were heavy and paused regularly, one hand on your hip, your shoulders rising and falling as you sighed. I'd sighed like that myself a thousand times since that night by the river. I knew how it felt. The sad weight of your heart. The gnawing guilt. The desperate desire to hide away from preying eyes and be alone. When a lady came up to you to ask about a book, you didn't smile and you barely spoke, just pointed up the spiral stairs with a finger that drooped. I almost ran over to grab it, to make it stand firm and to look in your eyes, urging you to forget what happened and live.

I didn't, of course. Talking to you at all would have made things worse, reminded you of things you were desperate to forget, and besides, I knew if I got too close I would cave, wanting to hold you to take your pain away and to tell you I love you, because I do, Alice, deeply. Instead, I said good-bye under my breath and turned to leave, and those five steps to the cold glass door were almost impossible to take. When I reached the place we'd kissed in the rain, I stood there for the longest time, remembering how your lips had burned against mine and how wrong it had been but how right it had felt, and then I was gone.

It goes without saying I'll never send this to you. It wouldn't be fair, and I'd be too afraid of someone reading it and discovering the truth of what happened between the three of us.

When it's finished, I'll tear it up and throw it away, just like I've done with all the rest. And when I get back to England and see you again, whenever that may be, I won't say anything that will make it impossible for you to move on. I won't tell you how much I love you or how scared I am of being without you or how I need to hide away from everyone because no one will ever compare to you. . . . I will simply let you go. True love is about sacrifice, after all, and if I want you to be free of the memory of Max, you need to be free of me.

Mr. Stubble and Mr. Bald have left. Light is fading and the traffic has died down, and there is just me and the parrot trapped in its cage. That's not how you're going to live, Bird Girl. Not on my account. Spread those strong wings of yours. Fly.

xxx

Acknowledgments

This book took a long time to get right, and I am grateful to my British editor, Fiona Kennedy, for giving me the time I needed, despite looming deadlines! Thank you for your patience, understanding, guidance, and editorial expertise. Thanks, too, to my brilliant American editor, Kate Sullivan: You are, quite simply, a dream to work with, and I feel very proud to be published by Little, Brown in the USA.

On a personal level, I would like to thank my mum, Shelagh Leech. You always make the time to read my stuff, and you're not afraid to tell me what you really think! Thanks to you and Dad for always, always being there. I am indebted to all my family and friends for their love, support, and the happiness they bring. In particular, I want to reserve my biggest and most heartfelt thanks for my wonderful husband, Steve. You did all the practical stuff that can be named—listened, proofread, advised—and hundreds of other things too special to write here. I couldn't have done it without you.